BOOK I

The Thief's Apprentice

Master DIPLEXITO and Mr. SCANT

The Thief's Apprentice

Bryan Methods

CAROLRHODA BOOKS
MINNEAPOLIS

Carolrhoda Books
A division of Lerner Publishing Group, Inc.
241 First Avenue North
Minneapolis, MN 55401 USA

For reading levels and more information, look up this title at www.lernerbooks.com.

Additional image: © iStockphoto.com/Roberto A Sanchez (paper background).

Main body text set in Bembo Std regular 12.5/17.
Typeface provided by Monotype Typography.

Library of Congress Cataloging-in-Publication Data

Names: Methods, Bryan, author.
Title: The thief's apprentice / by Bryan Methods.
Description: Minneapolis : Carolrhoda Books, [2016] | Summary: Oliver, the neurotic son of a wealthy British industrialist, discovers his family butler, Mr. Scant, is a notorious thief who soon takes on Oliver to become an apprentice vigilante.
Identifiers: LCCN 2015036023| ISBN 9781512405798 (lb : alk. paper) | ISBN 9781512408911 (eb pdf)
Subjects: | CYAC: Robbers and outlaws—Fiction. | Apprentices—Fiction. | Vigilantes—Fiction.
Classification: LCC PZ7.1.M49 Th 2016 | DDC [Fic]—dc23

LC record available at http://lccn.loc.gov/2015036023

Manufactured in the United States of America
1-39234-21111-3/30/2016

For a Moon Bunny, a
Dough Girl, and a Fish:
thank you for all the smiles!

And for Mum and Dad:
there can be no better
guides to living life well.

I

The Silent Battle

I remember the precise moment. The moment I learned a secret that had eluded the finest detectives of Scotland Yard—a secret the newspapers kept demanding to know yet nobody could tell them.

For months, a master thief had left the curators of museums up and down the country waking in cold sweats. Not a soul in England knew his identity, they said, and until that fateful moment, they were probably right. But no longer.

They called him the Ruminating Claw, this virtuoso of burglary. The razor-sharp talons he wore on one hand swiped away masterpiece after masterpiece, but all were returned mere days later. That made him a true criminal, according to the papers: he stole for the thrill of it, rather than to hoard his treasures or to sell them on. It seemed a mere game to him, dancing around the guards of London's finest museums and leaving the police looking like fools. The spokesman from Scotland Yard liked to say they were hot on his trail, but everyone knew there was no trail to follow. Nobody knew why he wore a sinister-looking metal claw on his right hand, but all agreed it made him dangerous.

But now I knew the truth, even if I could hardly believe it. The true identity of this fearsome Claw was Mr. Scant—my father's valet and our household butler. The tall, silver-haired old man who had to pick up my jacket if I dropped it, who was usually found standing respectfully just behind Father. My father being Mr. Sandleforth Diplexito, of Diplexito Engineering and Combustibles Ltd., Tunbridge Wells.

Perhaps, had I been clever enough, I could have guessed at the truth much earlier. But until the moment of realization came, I had thought Mr. Scant was nothing more than a particularly boring part of my endlessly boring life. He had always been a little frightening, with his sour looks and pointy eyebrows. His tone of voice always hinted he knew more than he let on. But if all gloomy old men with pointy eyebrows were to be marked as dangerous criminals, half my teachers and most of the congregation at church would have to be locked up. Then there was the fact that every report on the Ruminating Claw spoke of his remarkable agility and stealth, when Mr. Scant was positively ancient—at least sixty-five years old.

The moment I found out the truth came on a cold November night. I had crept out of bed to see if I could find where Mother had hidden my Christmas presents. Not something I would normally do, but this year, she had mentioned that, since I was now twelve and making my own way to school, a bicycle might be prudent. A bicycle wasn't an easy thing to hide, and even if she'd wrapped it up, it would have been easy to find. I had been jealously watching schoolmates send up clouds of dust with their skids and race each other down hills for months, so I decided to go for a late-night sneak.

After creeping to the long gallery, I saw something so bewilderingly unlikely, I wondered if I was actually still asleep. There, in the dead of night, was Mr. Scant. And there, on his right hand, was the famous claw, larger and even more vicious than it had looked in the newspaper. Instinct made me scurry behind the chaise longue, praying I hadn't been spotted. Only then did I begin to grasp what I had seen. And Mr. Scant had not been alone. Peering out from my hiding place, I saw that a man dressed all in black stood before him, brandishing a short, curved sword and wearing a cloth mask that hid all but his eyes. Mr. Scant faced him calmly, the golden claw raised at his opponent. On the tip of each finger was a long blade like a thin kitchen knife, with a complex arrangement of brass hinges and pistons running over the back of his hand.

The one and only photograph of the Claw—the halftone of him up on the pediment of the Fitzwilliam Museum—depicted him standing with the tips of the blades touching at his chin. The pose had given him his popular name, but entirely failed to capture the strange and evil look of the contraption itself, its eagerness to bite into the flesh of an enemy and stain itself red.

Such an enemy had clearly emerged. As I watched, the man in black surged forward, his blade catching the dim light from the streetlamp outside the window—but Mr. Scant reached out and grabbed the blade, stopping it dead. The claw had closed around the sword like the mandibles of some terrible insect, yet the loudest sound to be heard was the grunt from the man as he pulled his weapon loose.

This was the strangest part of all: the fight had been almost completely silent, as though the claw could cut the very sound from the air. Nothing was any louder than somebody setting down a knife and fork at the dinner table, even though at night, the tiniest sounds usually boom like church bells.

Mr. Scant looked almost lazy as he leaned away from vicious cuts at his throat, but the claw's blades flashed out, forcing the other man to leap back. They had an odd brightness to them: the curved sword gleamed, while the claw danced with soft luminescence.

As Mr. Scant danced around his opponent, I remembered Mother's remark that when going about his butler's duties, Mr. Scant crossed the house silently as a cat. She had once gone so far as to scold him for creeping up on her—which was the talk of the household for days afterwards. Then there was the time when the farm boy almost dropped one of the big pails of milk, only for Mr. Scant to rush down the steps to catch it without spilling a drop. At the time, I reasoned it was a case of being in the right place at the right time, but in truth, Mr. Scant had moved like a viper. Could I have guessed at his secret from that? It would have taken greater detective skills than mine. And I would say my detective skills are roughly average for a boy of twelve.

The masked man began to grow desperate. He aimed blow after blow at Mr. Scant's head, but the claw caught every one, making no more than a soft scraping sound. When the stranger leapt at him, Mr. Scant dodged the thrust of his sword, then grabbed the man with his left hand and flipped him over his shoulder onto the old sofa. I feared my own breathing would betray me, that my heart pounded so loudly the sound was pouring from my ears. But at the same time, I was mesmerized.

With an abruptness that made me feel sick, the fight ended. The man must have decided the best way to upset Mr. Scant would be to make a lot of noise. But the moment he took a deep breath, Mr. Scant was upon him. When the blades flashed and plunged into the soft part beneath the man's ribs, I was afraid his opponent had drawn his last breath. But Mr. Scant had curled the claw into a fist and punched all the air out of the man before he could make a sound.

Like a puppet with its strings cut, the man slumped over Mr. Scant's shoulder. Silent as ever, the old man stood and quickly made for the main staircase.

What the Ruminating Claw planned to do with his victim, I had no way to know. Nor did I dare risk following him to find out. I felt almost as though I had been the one who'd been punched and sat with my back to the chaise longue trying to catch my breath. I tried to think, but my head was the net of a fishing boat, dropped onto the deck. The day's catch had spilled everywhere.

A dangerous criminal lived here, in my home—a criminal with the keys to every room, whose proper place was within stabbing distance of Father's back. And what I could do, now that I knew this secret, I had not the faintest idea.

II

No Liar

The next day passed slowly. Excruciatingly slowly. I couldn't sleep at all, and when Penny the maid came to rouse me in the morning, I felt as though someone had pushed cotton wool behind my eyeballs. The feeling didn't go away at school, either. My arms and legs seemed to crackle with a kind of electric power, only instead of energizing me, each spark added to the fear of what was waiting for me at home.

Though I had first wanted to share my discovery, I decided not to tell anybody at school. They would only laugh at me, or demand proof, and nobody would believe me, except Bert Simmons. He believed anything anybody said as long as they nodded as they spoke. And even if one of my friends would accept the truth, what would that mean for my family?

I couldn't risk getting the wrong person involved. For all I knew, the old monster had allies every-where. One time, Mr. Beards, of Beards and Binns Financial Services and Dirigibles Ltd., had called for dinner with his family, and his daughter Gerty said she saw a monstrous face in the window. When she fainted, Mr. Scant had been there in an instant to steady her. I remembered the moment well, because Father had given Mr. Scant a slap on the back and a quiet, "Good show," which was more praise than he had ever given me. Nobody had believed Gerty had really seen anything; after all, Gerty was a bit of an "odd duck," as Mrs. George put it, and never chewed with her mouth closed no matter how much her mother whispered to her. But what if Gerty had been right, and some nasty little criminal accomplice had been perched outside, trying to get his master's attention?

By lunchtime, I imagined everybody to be a potential enemy. Mr. Scant was always the first in the household to rise and the last to sleep, so who knew how many people he could meet with while we slept? Did that "Ganymede Club for Gentlemen's Gentlemen" he went to really exist? Maybe he was in league with that nasty-looking brother of Peter

Clephane's, or with Mr. Prigg, the games master—and if I told them, it would get back to Mr. Scant. Who knew what he would do to me then?

So I kept my silence, but the effort meant I could think of nothing else. A dense fog had surrounded me, soaking into my woolly brain and weighing it down. If I had for brief, happy moments imagined being hailed as the hero of the day after telling a friendly policeman what I knew, I soon realized this outcome was impossible. The Ruminating Claw was uncatchable, after all. He thought nothing of waltzing in and out of the Victoria and Albert, and considered the National Gallery his own property. He had flummoxed the famous guards of the Tower of London not once but twice, stealing and then later returning the Sword of Mercy from its place amongst the Crown Jewels. But that didn't mean he was a phantom or could turn into mist—fine, upstanding policemen had been injured trying to catch him. Now I myself had seen how he could fight.

What had become of the man he had bested? I kept returning to that question. Had the masked man met a terrible end and been dumped in the woods? The thought was absolutely the reason I fumbled the ball when Chudley passed it to me during games.

Not long after I got home, I saw Mr. Scant again. Every Thursday after school, I had to endure a tutoring session with Mr. Ibberts in Father's library. If concentrating in school had been a challenge, I had little hope of being able to listen to one of Mr. Ibberts's rambling sentences through to the end. Every time I heard a door closing or a floorboard creak, I turned to check for a maniacal butler bursting into the room. Unfortunately, when I laid my head on my hands to watch the shadows under the door, Mr. Ibberts noticed.

Without warning, he slammed his book onto the desk, making me sit up in alarm. "Am I keeping you awake, Master Oliver?"

"No sir. Sorry, sir. Actually, I think this might be the most awake I've ever been in one of your lessons."

"Then perhaps you can remind me which young pretender to the throne I just described?"

"I . . ." It was then I noticed that Mr. Ibberts's book had stayed open on the page from which he had been reading. "Lambert . . . Simnel, I believe?" I chanced, reading from the title.

Mr. Ibberts gave a strange kind of grunt as he snatched the book up.

I tried to look contrite. "I'm sorry, sir. I'm just a little distracted."

"Whatever frivolity your little head is stuck in, I sincerely doubt it merits more interest than the history of our great isle."

"Well, sir, I think maybe your idea of what's interesting is a bit different from mine." I knew at once I had gone too far, because Mr. Ibberts's ears went red. "Sorry, sir," I said. "I didn't mean to be rude. I just have a lot I have to think about."

"Kings and princes had whipping boys to take their punishments for them, but you have no such luxuries, Master Oliver, I warn you!"

"I remember you saying so before, sir. Lots of times."

"I ought to . . . to . . ." Mr. Ibberts began.

"Tell Father? Do you really think he'd care?" I sighed, laying my head down on my arms. "He'd just tell you it's your job to deal with me."

At that moment, just as I let down my guard, the door opened behind me with a quiet click.

"Please forgive my interruption."

I sat bolt upright but didn't dare turn to look. Mr. Scant's gravelly voice was unmistakable.

"Not at all, not at all," said Mr. Ibberts, obviously

flustered at the thought of someone overhearing our exchange.

The rumbling voice came again. "I was sent for a book. It will only take a moment to find."

"Please," said Mr. Ibberts. "We were just having a brief, ah . . . *break* from the lesson. I was impressing on Master Oliver the importance of concentration."

"Indeed," said Mr. Scant, coming around the desk to regard me with interest. "I've heard it said there are no dull lessons, only dull children. But you are not dull, are you, Master Oliver?"

"I . . . No. No, Mr. Scant."

Mr. Scant gave a nod, then seemed to find the book he required without so much as a glance at the shelf. Mr. Ibberts looked very interested in how shaken I was, and I could already tell he hoped to use my fear of Mr. Scant against me in future lessons. Once Mr. Scant took his leave and we were alone again, Mr. Ibberts raised his textbook again with a smug flourish, and I made sure to stay obedient for the rest of the session.

Afterwards, I went to check on Mother. I found her in the long gallery, reading the book Mr. Scant had fetched, with her elderly maid Mrs. Winton hovering behind her. The scoundrel himself was nowhere in sight.

"Why are you looking at me like that?" Mother asked.

"Like what?"

"Like you're surprised to see me?"

"I'm not surprised to see you, Mother. Just . . . I'm happy you're safe."

She peered at me over her spectacles. "Funny rabbit," she remarked.

"I'm not a rabbit."

Back in my room, I pondered what to do. If I said nothing to Mother and Father, and then Mr. Scant did something terrible when I could have warned them, how could I ever forgive myself? This was a situation that could not last. The best course of action would be to find evidence of Mr. Scant's wrongdoings as quickly as possible. If I discovered something incriminating, Father might even be impressed by my initiative—though that didn't sound very likely, even in my own head. Nevertheless, I decided to go on the hunt for any evidence of Mr. Scant's secret identity.

With Father busy at work, it was a good bet that Mr. Scant would head for the kitchens, where he could easily hear the bell if Mother wanted him.

Heading in that direction, I found him sooner than I expected, catching sight of his rounded coattails as I made my way down the central staircase. Assuming that the rest of him was attached, I hurried to follow. He truly was quieter than any cat: I could only follow him by watching the swing of the doors he had gone through, and even then, Mr. Scant closed them without so much as a click.

I reached the stone steps leading to the kitchens and staff quarters. As I made my way down, I could hear Mrs. George's voice booming away. That was good—she would cover up the sound of my investigation. Stopping on the bottom step, I peered around the corner toward the kitchens and then paused. "If Mr. Scant is ahead of me," I mumbled to myself, "why hasn't Mrs. George said hello?"

With grim inevitability, a gloved hand landed on my shoulder.

Stopping myself from yelping only by shoving the greater part of my fist into my mouth, I whirled around. Mr. Scant, of course, had been in the other part of the basement corridor, the section leading to the staff quarters. His thin lips were pursed even tighter than usual—and those were lips framed by the wrinkles of a lifetime of pursing.

"Master Oliver," he intoned, one bushy eyebrow raising like a drawbridge.

One of Mrs. George's booming laughs from the kitchen gave the moment the feeling of a farce, but no part of this was funny. I had put myself in competition with a criminal renowned for his stealth and had unsurprisingly fallen short of the mark.

"Is there something I can do for you?" asked Mr. Scant.

"I came to ask for a sugar cube before dinner!" I blurted.

The scrutiny from Mr. Scant's eyes intensified, and it had already been at least three times more scrutiny than anyone ought to have to suffer. "Ha ha, you remember, I'm sure, M-Mr. Scant," I babbled. "Mother likes her l–little . . . little joke about me. 'Oh, he doesn't have a sweet tooth, he has a mouth full of them.' Ha! Oh, Mother. Yes, and Mrs. George gives me sugar sometimes! You've seen, I'm sure you've seen. Remember, I used to eat the ones that were there in case guests might want them in their tea? And Father said I should have a nosebag. Bit unkind, but maybe he's right, ha ha! Ha."

Hasty as it had been, my excuse was not wholly terrible. The main question was whether or not Mr.

Scant would remember that three or four years had passed since I last asked Mrs. George for such a childish treat. His eyes continued to pierce into mine, his hand still on my shoulder. Despite the lightness of his grip, that hand paralyzed me as surely as an iron maiden. Was my babbling too much? Would he see right through me and decide I was more trouble than I was worth, that the corridor's stone walls would look good with a nice new lick of dribbly red paint?

After an eternity, Mr. Scant lifted his hand. I felt like Atlas must have when Heracles took up his burden. Waiting long enough to be sure Mr. Scant hadn't released me just to make it easier to chop me up, I stepped timorously toward the kitchen. The moment I did, Mr. Scant spoke. "By all means, Master Oliver, try your luck with Mrs. George."

"I will," I squeaked, and sidled away slowly, in the way I imagine I would if I fell into the bear pit at the zoo. Apposite, then, that another growl stopped me two steps later.

"Ah, and you need not worry, Master Oliver: I would never dream of letting your mother in on your little secret. A gentleman's gentleman is always capable of discretion. Especially when keeping a secret is clearly the wisest course."

I looked back at him slowly, to see whether the words were a prelude to a deeply unpleasant bit of violence, but Mr. Scant remained quite still. He loomed in the basement dark, expecting a response. He was rather good at looming.

"I quite agree," I croaked. In the last minute, I had managed to blurt, babble, squeak, and now croak at the man. If my survival depended on being able to speak normally, I was in trouble.

"Then we have an understanding," he said. "A good gentleman never tells a lie, but also knows when it is unnecessary to say anything at all."

I swallowed. Was this a test? Part of me bristled with anger, because Mr. Scant was clearly enjoying my discomfort, but the rest of me shushed it before I could say anything. Instead, I nodded.

As I did, Mr. Scant held up a finger. "Ah! I do believe I can hear your father's motorcar, Master Oliver. The engine produces a very distinctive note. Please excuse me." With that, he swept past me and up the stairs.

"I . . . yes," I said to the empty corridor.

In a daze, I shuffled to the kitchen. It seemed wrong not to, now. As I stepped inside, Mrs. George funneled her chatter into a loud coo and hurried over. "Master Oliver! Been a while since we saw you down here!" She swiped at the flour caking her apron in an attempt to tidy herself up, but the apron was so thickly coated that a cloud expanded around her. That may have explained why everything looked a bit hazy, but not why my head was spinning. "What can we do you for? Are you all right, Duck? You look a bit pale."

"I'm fine, just dizzy all of a sudden." I was in a muddle over what was truth and what I had invented. "I just, erm . . . I was after a lump of—"

"Ooh, you look like you've seen a ghost. I'm not that pale with the flour, am I? Am I, girls?"

"No, miss," chorused the twins, who were rolling pastry.

"I shouldn't think someone made as solidly as I am would ever be mistook for a ghost, anyway," Mrs. George said cheerfully.

"You look thick as ever, miss," said Meg, and giggled with her sister.

"Do you need a sit down and some water, Duck?" asked Mrs. George, bringing over a little stool.

"Water would be nice," I said, sitting down. "All of a sudden I'm feeling . . . What's the word?"

"Dizzy?" Mrs. George put in.

"Peculiar?" suggested Penny.

"Wobbly?" proposed Meg.

"Discombobulated," I said.

"That was going to be my next guess," said Meg.

I gave Penny a look. "And don't say I've always looked peculiar to you. I know you were going to."

Penny turned her nose up. "I'd never dream it!"

That exchange seemed to amuse the sisters further. I always suspected they had some sort of private joke about me between them, but I knew they'd never tell me even if they did.

"Here's water, Duck. What's brought you downstairs?"

"Actually, I was looking for Mr. Scant," I said. "Bumped into him outside."

"Not too hard, I hope. Made all of elbows, that man!" Mrs. George brayed like a donkey at her little joke. "Now, how about a taste of sugar? Don't you go pretending yer all grown up. Never too old for a little treat—'til yer gnashers start going black, anyhow. What was it you was after ole Scant for?"

"Just . . . had to ask him something."

"Hmm! Now, don't let the man frighten you, hear? Might have a face that's like to make that 'orrible Mr. Scrooge run off and hide behind the nearest orphan, but there's a good heart in that ribcage."

"Do you think so?"

"I do indeed. And I'll have you know I am an excellent judge of such things, thank you very much! Here we are—one sugar lump. Do *not* let it spoil yer appetite, or I shall give you something to really be afeared of. If I hear reports there've been any *I'm-full-ups* or *I-can't-manage-another-bite-Mummy-dearests*, you will have my rolling pin across the top of yer noggin. Finish up every scrap, even if you have to store it in your cheeks, hear?"

"I will. Thank you," I said, taking what she proffered—two misshapen little sugar lumps rather than the neat cubes I preferred. Or had preferred when I was small. "Mrs. George?"

"Not getting any more'n that from me, Duck. Them tarts are strictly for—"

"It's not that. I just wanted to ask . . . have you ever thought there's more to Mr. Scant than we know?"

"Well, that depends what you know, my duck. A lot going on *up here* with that one." She tapped the side of her head. "Plenty he'll never show in front of that lot upstairs, I don't mind telling you. But that Scant's a good man, and as stiff as he looks. Never tells a lie, either."

"He just said so, actually."

"And it was no lie, neither!" Mrs. George sent more flour tumbling from her apron as she laughed and slapped her hand on the counter. "No, but my dear, you mustn't be afeared of his sort. Everyone has their way of going through life, and his way is straight down the middle, no nonsense, no fuss. And we could all learn a thing or two from that. Couldn't we, girls?"

"Yes, miss," the twins said again.

"He does have them scary hands, though," Penny added.

"I still say he got 'em in the fighting out in Africa," said Meg. When she saw my inquisitive look, she explained in a hushed voice, "He took his gloves off once, in here, when I got something on them by accident."

"All covered in scars!" said Penny.

"*I'm* the one telling this story! You hush up!"

"That's enough of that," Mrs. George said, "and when I say enough's enough, it is *enough*. Master Oliver will think we're gossips. Who can say how a fella gets scars on his hand? Maybe he put it in a fire when he was a babe? No use in making guesses."

I popped a sugar lump into my mouth, crunching it between my teeth, and felt the fear that had filled my bones begin to fade. There was no way to feel nervous around Mrs. George: once you stepped into her kitchen, troubles ran from the cannon fire of her laugh. Even if those troubles included imminent death by impalement on metal claws.

"The thing is, Mrs. George . . ." I began, but wasn't sure what the thing was, so started again. "What I'm *thinking* is that if you have things you don't want people to know, maybe the . . . the way you do that is to make the world *think* you're a . . . straight-and-narrow sort of fellow, who would never do anything strange . . ."

"Oh, my dear duck," said Mrs. George, "there is not a single person in this world I think could *never* do anything strange."

Mrs. George could not have known how much better she had made me feel. That huge laugh of hers sent my fears flying away over the horizon. Coming home from school, I had doubted I would ever sleep again, but as I settled down into bed that night, I felt safe. Here, in my father's house, I lay surrounded by people I knew and trusted to protect me. As for Mr. Scant, perhaps he only wanted to keep his secret safe. I even entertained the possibility that he was more afraid of me than I was of him.

That notion shattered when a hand clamped over my mouth and jolted me awake, stifling what would surely have been the very manliest of screams.

III
He Who Does Not Toil

I knew I had no chance of wresting myself free. Nor was Mr. Scant going to release me if I kept on trying to yell for help through his palm. So as I settled from panic into a kind of miserable, shrinking fear, I did my best to keep still—though my shoulders had decided they were going to tremble and were sticking with that plan no matter what.

When I fell silent, Mr. Scant released his palm from across my face, the cold look in his eyes warning me not to make a sound. I tried my best to gasp for breath in silence.

What Mr. Scant did next left me mystified: he stepped back and made a downward gesture, indicating his person with both hands, and raised his eyebrows meaningfully. "Here I am" was the obvious meaning, but why I had to be shown this in the middle of the night, scared at least seven-eighths to death, I hadn't the faintest. Then, without another word, Mr. Scant turned and left.

I stared at the door. Five or six hours must have passed while I sat there. A vision of a huge metal claw dashing it to splinters played over and over in my mind, like the moving picture in one of those spinning zoetropes. In all that time, however, the clock on the bedside table only changed from 3:17 to 3:33. I thought this was nonsense, but when the sun didn't rise, I had to accept it.

Eventually, I settled back down onto my pillow, and the next thing I knew, Meg was bringing in my clothes for the day and calling in a bright voice that it was time to wake up. Compared with her sister Penny, Meg had a considerably less gentle approach to the morning routine: if I didn't get out of bed, she liked to roll me off the edge of the mattress. So I sat up, rubbing my eyes. That unreliable sun had at last found its way up into the sky, its feeble winter light exploring my room. I let out a loud groan and held my head.

"Not sick again are you, Master Oliver?" asked Meg.

"I don't think so."

"Y'look like y'did that time you got that bad food at the party."

"The bad canapés at Peter Clephane's birthday? Urgh. And then Macclesfield looking smug all the rest of that term because he hadn't come."

"Maybe them fancy foods aren't meant for schoolboys," said Meg with a prim smile, laying out my school uniform and leaving me to wash and dress.

As expected, Mr. Scant stood in wait for me when I went downstairs, lurking behind the arrangement of newspaper and fingers that was all we ever saw of Father at the breakfast table. As I took my seat, I felt like a field mouse watched by a hungry owl, not daring to look away in case the bird swooped in for a silent kill. In the end, I almost made a mess of my egg and soldiers by trying to dip them without taking my eyes off Mr. Scant.

Suddenly, those strigine eyes of his flickered downward. This was no loss of nerve on his part, but rather an instruction: his eyes were leading mine toward Father's newspaper. Frowning, I read the headline: A THIRD VETO FOR RUSSELL, it proclaimed, which like most headlines meant nothing whatsoever. But underneath, in smaller characters, I found what I was meant to see: THE RUMINATING CLAW, ONCE AGAIN, STRIKES!!

I shot to my feet, which made my chair fall over. Father flicked the corner of the paper down and eyeballed me in irritation. "What the devil is the matter?" he demanded.

"Nothing. Sorry, Father," I said in a small voice, as Mother helped me pick up the chair. "I was just surprised by something. A fly."

Father rolled his eyes before flicking the paper back up. "Scared of a fly . . ." I gave him a hurt look, but only the headlines could see it.

The body of the article was not, as would have been most convenient, on the front page—I had to make do with a short summary. I tried to read without squinting or leaning closer, as Mother was already giving me an inquisitive look. "The criminal known as the Ruminating Claw has struck again in London's National Portrait Gallery," the article read. "This report was rushed to the presses after the crime took place in the small hours of the morning. Reported stolen was a painting by the Dutch"— I wondered for a moment if the painting had been a collaborative effort before realizing the sentence continued on page five. Unwilling to disturb Father again, I could read no further, but the message was clear nonetheless.

When I looked back to Mr. Scant, he raised his eyebrows, and I hoped the look I gave in return showed him I understood his message. He had woken me to demonstrate he was not involved in this latest theft. The Ruminating Claw had struck—and Mr. Scant had not been present for the crime. Even if it was entirely possible to travel to London and return to Tunbridge Wells in a single night, Mr. Scant had chosen the hour with a purpose: it fell evenly between sunset and sunrise, giving him no time to get to London and back without his absence being noticed in the household.

For a fleeting moment, I thought this meant I'd been mistaken and that Mr. Scant was not the Claw after all, but I quickly realized that could not be the case. True, Mr. Scant could not have been responsible for last night's theft, but crucially, he knew about it before it was reported. The other message Mr. Scant had conveyed to me, when I thought about it, frightened me even more: he knew I thought he was the Claw. He knew I had discovered his secret.

A day at school promised some relief from the burdens of home—a very unusual feeling. While I was happy to escape, though, I also feared for Mother. After I put on my blazer and cap at the door, I gave her a long hug, which made her laugh and say, "You won't get out of school that way." I tried to deliver a menacing look to Mr. Scant before letting go, but he was busy preparing Father's overcoat, and even had he seen me, most likely he wouldn't have cared very much.

The school day was long. Judner's School took as its motto *Qui non Laborat non Floreat*, which meant "He who does not toil does not flourish," but most of the teachers looked the other way as long as you at least pretended. All through Double Science, I planned what to do when I got home: acting as though nothing had happened would be easiest, which was probably what Mr. Scant wanted. But knowing a criminal lived in the house, with Mother and Father all unawares, would eat away at me inside. Yet I was also afraid to tell them. Father would march up to Mr. Scant, of course, and demand an explanation. I dreaded to think what the Ruminating Claw would do, confronted like that. He could be as dangerous as Jack the Ripper. He could *be* Jack the Ripper, for all I knew. The thought of his plan for *me* gave me enough to worry about, though I took a small amount of comfort from knowing that if Mr. Scant had wanted to do away with me, he would have done it the previous night. One does not give riddles to a boy that one is about to tie up in a burlap sack and dump in a river.

Which was not to say that should I provoke him, he would not change his mind.

At lunch, I almost fell asleep in my apple and rhubarb custard. My friend Chudley gave me a poke in the ribs so savage that it almost made me fall off the bench, and everyone laughed.

"Stop that," I said.

"Up all night revising for Osbaldeston's test?"

I blinked. "We have a test?"

Chudley laughed. "Oh, dear. I think you're in trouble."

A bad mark on a Latin test might have worried me the week before, but just then, it was the least of my concerns. I needed to gather information. Carefully.

As it was Friday, I had no tuition session after school, so I could start as soon as I got home. Even so, I found myself trudging to the house at a snail's pace. Once home, I went straight to my room and thought hard about whether I should give up on the day and go to bed.

Staring at my reflection in the mirror of my dresser, however, I realized hiding myself away would be the most intolerable thing. I would surely go mad if I tried it.

I didn't know what I hoped to discover through my investigation, but if I wanted to survive, the best thing would be to find solid evidence for Mr. Scant's true identity.

When I checked on Mother, she informed me we had guests that evening. Father's business partners, Mr. Beards and Mr. Binns of Beards and Binns Financial Services and Dirigibles Ltd., would be calling for dinner. That meant we would eat earlier than usual, so the men could retire to Father's study afterward. Mr. Scant would be attending to them, supplying the brandies and cigars and anything else they might want. It seemed a good opportunity to observe Mr. Scant without being seen myself, so I hatched a plan.

I excused myself after the cheese course, saying I had been given a lot of prep this weekend. But instead of going to my room to practice Latin declensions, I slipped into Father's study. The men always went there to discuss business after dinner, which—from what I had managed to glimpse through the doors— mostly meant drinking brandy and arguing about the rules of a dice game. Mother said this was how the world of business worked.

I slid behind the thick curtains on the far side of the room from the door, and for some half an hour, stood in wait. Eventually, I realized that sitting behind the curtain was no less sneaky than standing behind it, so I settled down onto the floor. Just as I began to wish I had brought a book, burly voices drifted in from the other side of the door, and I scrambled to my feet before burly bodies followed.

The gist of the terribly serious discussion was that Mr. Beards wanted to change the supplier of some part or other Father needed in his engines. Mr. Beards was very keen on the idea, while Father stressed the advantages of the existing deal. Even if they could save some money in the short term, Father said, they would lose solid and well-established connections. It was all very business-y.

"But Sandleforth, you must see that Tenterton and the whole bally lot are reliant on you now," said Mr. Beards, stopping to wheeze, as was his habit. "You can't imagine for a moment the bounders are in any position to walk away. They need us!"

"Maybe so, but we've spent a long time establishing trust across the board. If we abandon Tenterton, what stops the rest from thinking their heads are next on the block? That maybe they should hike their prices to get all they can out of the deal before we cut them off?"

Mr. Binns weighed in: "Perhaps the notion that their heads will be next on the block is not such a bad one for them to hold." He had a smooth, lazy voice, as though his words mixed with the wax in his pointy moustache on their way out. "*Feared than loved*—and all that."

"I'm against it," said Father. "What we need to do is to *hint* to Sykes that this alternative deal exists. Give him just a whiff of it. Then he might want to start thinking about our arrangement. Just don't scare him off. Daft sod's already more skittish than a sparrow."

And so it went on. Emboldened by boredom, I chanced a peek out from behind my curtain to scan for Mr. Scant. I spotted him at once, attending to Father by the writing desk. The study was longer than most train carriages, so a fair distance stretched between my spot behind the curtain and where the men were talking. Whatever I hoped to see Mr. Scant doing, I knew I wasn't about to see it from across the room, so slipped out into the open.

As the universe and all the Fates apparently hold some grudge against me, the buckle of my slipper got tangled in the tassels at the bottom of the curtain. When I felt a tug, I spun around, afraid I had been caught, and as my foot failed to come with me, there was nothing to do but get better acquainted with the carpet.

While I fell, Mr. Scant—without so much as a look in my direction—crossed swiftly to the drinks cabinet and let the tray door fall open with a loud bang.

"What the devil, Scant?" Father barked.

"My apologies, sir. I thought it a good time for some Armagnac, but the hinge came loose. I will see to it that it is repaired."

After a short pause, Father grunted and said, "Armagnac does sound agreeable. But no more disruptions, if you please. Apologies, gentlemen."

"Not at all—gratifying to see he's human after all," said Mr. Beards, with a merry little chuckle that descended into another wheeze. "I shall have to tell Deidre. She's convinced that valet of yours is beyond fault."

Mr. Binns gave an amused little snort. "You're lucky you found that new man of yours. I'll need to find another soon, I'm sure. My sweet, sweet wife gives a member of our staff the chuck every week, or so it seems . . ."

As he turned to prepare the drinks, Mr. Scant's eyes flicked in my direction. So fiery was his gaze, I worried the carpet beneath me would be reduced to ash. Then he began distributing glasses, brandishing the decanter in those deft criminal's hands of his. Feeling rather undignified, I sat up and untangled my shoe. Perhaps, if I managed to sneak out with no more fuss, Mr. Scant and I could reach a gentlemen's agreement: none of this had ever happened, and there was no need for anyone to disembowel anyone else.

Hoping beyond hope this might be the case, I managed to crawl halfway to the door before Mr. Scant's shadow fell across me. He excused himself, saying he ought to check on the fire in the living room, then strode past me and opened the doors. When he turned, I realized he was standing to one side so that I could scamper out in front of him. I hurried to make the most of my opportunity.

Unfortunately, my scramble for freedom left me right underneath a very unimpressed Ruminating Claw. I froze like a baby rabbit under the jaws of a hungry fox. For a moment we were still, until I smiled diffidently, at which point the thief seized my wrist and pulled me to my feet before marching me into the music room.

"Master Oliver, I see that we are going to have difficulties," said Mr. Scant.

"If you harm a hair on my head, Father will hear of it!"

"If I am to harm you, Master Oliver, do you imagine I would leave you in a state to tell your father anything? Perhaps you should reflect on how rare it may or *may not* be for boys to fall through the ice of frozen ponds while walking home from school, never to be heard from again."

I didn't know what to say to that, and I wasn't sure the tight feeling in my throat would let me say anything anyway.

"Now, you can stop looking at me that way. That pout is not becoming," Mr. Scant went on, taking a moment to listen for movement in the hallway. "You were not meant to see what you saw, Master Oliver. It puts me in a difficult position. But if I meant to garrote you with the piano strings, I would have already done so. Middle C is particularly good for the job."

"Why haven't you?" I managed.

"I do not consider it to be to my advantage. But if you continue in your attempts to convince me otherwise, that may change. Was my message last night not clear enough?"

For the first time since Mr. Scant had pulled me into the music room, I could meet his eye. I drew myself up. "It was clear."

"Then you should know I was not the thief you seem to think you have discovered."

"But that's not right at all. Not being there last night doesn't mean you're not the Claw."

That stopped him. He cocked his head for all the world like a pigeon in the park that thinks you have a fistful of bread crumbs. "If I may be so bold, Master Oliver—may I ask your meaning?"

"You wanted me to see that you were *here* when the Claw stole that painting. Which I understood. You couldn't have been at the National Portrait Gallery or stolen the painting. But . . . you *knew* to wake me. You *knew* what would be in the news this morning. That means you knew the Claw was going to strike! So either you are *one* Claw and there are others, or . . ."

Mr. Scant raised one eyebrow. "Or?"

"Or you're the Claw—and the Claw isn't the one doing the stealing."

For an instant, I thought I might have seen the edge of a smile on Mr. Scant's lips, in the same way one *almost* sees the movement of a clock's hour hand. He contemplated me as if for the first time, then said, "When your father's guests leave tonight, wait for twenty minutes. And then, if you would be so kind, I should like you to join me here again."

I swallowed. "What happens if I don't?"

"I would advise against finding out."

Once again, he turned on his heel and left me. And that was that. Lips dry and knuckles blanched, I withdrew to my room. Settling into my soft chair, I picked up my book about a jungle explorer, while Father and his guests went on with their meeting. After a very, very long time spent staring at the same page, I heard voices and crept to the top of the stairs to listen. A woman was speaking with the declamatory voice of a trained actress, and I knew at once it was Mrs. Binns, here to collect her husband.

"You know how I feel about being made to wait!" she snapped. She was a severe woman, with a face more pinched than the strictest schoolmarm and a smile far more terrible than her frown. I was glad to be out of the way, upstairs.

"Coming, dear!" I heard Mr. Binns call, before the men appeared, laughing together.

"Yes, yes, important men do love to dawdle," Mrs. Binns remarked with a sniff. "It's how the others know they are important, and the sole thing they have practiced to perfection."

"Very well observed, my darling," said Mr. Binns, and a general bustling commenced as he and Mr. Beards took their leave. Mr. Scant would be down there, quietly helping the men into their coats. After Mr. Beards wheezed his way through some goodbyes and Mrs. Binns told her husband off for smelling of cigar smoke, the guests finally departed. Once the door was closed behind them, I heard Mother speak.

"She does like her witticisms, that Thomasina. They strike me as a little old-fashioned."

Father laughed. "Perhaps next time you should tell her to refrain."

"I wouldn't dare!" said Mother. "I don't want my head bitten off. You can tell who's in charge of that marriage."

"Come now, we both know the wife is the one in charge of every marriage. Only you all pretend we're too soft in the head to know it. And you don't like that Mrs. Binns doesn't play the game."

"That sounded dangerously close to a witticism, my darling."

Mother and Father had started up the stairs, so I slipped back to my room. Instead of picking up my book again, I took out my pocket watch and began counting down the twenty minutes Mr. Scant had stipulated. The watch tormented me with its tiny, taunting clicks, and I soon came to learn that twenty minutes looked uncannily like the rise and fall of a mountain. But when the time came, I almost wished it hadn't.

I crept downstairs to the music room, and when I opened the door, it was no surprise whatsoever to see the old man standing beside what was clearly the stolen painting from the museum, covered by a sheet.

"Well then, Master Oliver," he said, "let us begin."

IV
The Gallery

W hat would Mother say, I thought to myself, if she found out what I was up to?

We left behind the streetlamps of Tunbridge Wells. The town gave way to fields and hedgerows, which the relentless carriage wheels then plucked away, one by one. So little light was left in the world on this starless night—only the frighteningly small pool from the carriage lamps.

I tried to remember if I had ever been so far from home without Mother. There had been the school trip to the muddy field where the Battle of Hastings had been fought—not, in fact, in Hastings, but in the conveniently named town of Battle. Tonight's destination was farther from home than that, though. And of course a school trip was not quite the same as a clandestine mission to commit a crime. What was that crime? Not theft, only trespass. We were on the way to London to break into the National Portrait Gallery.

Mr. Scant brooded silently, running one bony finger down his chin over and over again. It was a habit he broke only when another carriage or a motorcar passed, at which point he pulled his scarf over his face. The carriage curtains were barely open, so I thought this was a bit much. But I would never risk saying so, especially with Mr. Scant so still and quiet that I nearly believed he himself had sucked all the light out of the sky. Odder still: beneath his scarf and plain inverness cape, he still wore his valet's tailcoat.

The coachman for our journey was a sharp-eyed man of perhaps thirty. I had never seen his face before, and it was not a face one could easily forget. He bore enough scars across it that anybody could tell at a glance he lived in an entirely different world from the one I knew. He didn't so much as acknowledge me, and I found myself quite relieved about that.

The thieving, it seemed, had already been done. In Mr. Scant's possession was the missing painting. And indeed, Mr. Scant said, he had stolen it. But only after another party had stolen it first.

"I did the deed during the forty minutes that your father was at the bank and your mother was taking her bath," he informed me. "Naturally, that did not involve a trip to the National Portrait Gallery and back. No, I intercepted those thieves and relieved them of their stolen goods."

Where this had taken place and how Mr. Scant had known where to find these villains remained a mystery.

For the umpteenth time since getting into the carriage, I wondered what I was doing there. When Mr. Scant had said he wanted me to accompany him as he returned the painting, terror ran fingers all up and down my spine, but that didn't mean I was surprised. I couldn't have predicted where we would go, but somehow I had been certain that Mr. Scant meant to take me away from everything I knew and trusted. Once I went to the music room, everything felt mechanical, as if I were a windup toy with no choice but to walk forward, out of the house, and down the path and into the old growler carriage waiting outside the gates. It wasn't as though I could have refused. I no longer dealt with Father's valet, the household butler. I dealt with the Ruminating Claw.

And now here we were, almost at our destination.

London began to rip its way out of the countryside, bringing its brightness with it. This did not fill me with eagerness. The excited little boy I had once been, the Oliver who stood on his seat to get the first glimpse of the city, was long gone. If gold had ever really paved these streets, as Dick Whittington once dreamed, it had long been buried under muck or pried loose and pawned.

Soon, the streets grew wider and notably less bumpy. There was no chance to enjoy the smoothness, though: our scarred coachman spurred the horses to a frightening pace. Lamplights flashed again and again past our windows, as if we were a ship passing a manic lighthouse. I gripped at the leather of my seat, thinking about what Mr. Scant had told me when I said I was afraid we would be caught. "To get away, a person need only disappear upwards. Remember that, Master Oliver."

In an attempt to settle my nerves, I let out a little laugh and said to Mr. Scant, "London, eh? I usually only come with Father's friends. Business partners, I should probably say. I have to pretend I'm having a wonderful time at some horrible opera or something. The last one was about a fat woman in a sack and a fat man with a pillow up the back of his shirt to make him look like a hunchback. They went on for hours, right in each other's faces. That was the last time father smacked me with the slipper—when I nearly fell asleep. Not my fault! 'No son of mine will be a philistine!' Smack, smack. I can't help it. Why can't we go and see shows about flying boys and pirates like everyone else? 'Frivolous nonsense.' Puh!"

Mr. Scant apparently wasn't in the mood for idle chatter. He went on staring out of the window.

"Don't want to sound ungrateful, though," I added.

I couldn't really compare this with a trip to the capital with my parents, of course. Those trips hadn't involved any criminal acts. The plan, according to Mr. Scant, was straightforward: we would evade the guards of the National Portrait Gallery and put the painting back where it belonged. Simple. According to him, at any rate. Why he wanted me at his side wasn't clear, but I was too afraid to refuse.

Had the journey taken a hundred years, making me roughly the same age as Mr. Scant, I don't think I would ever have felt prepared. As it was, when he drew his scarf up over his face and said, "We're here," I felt my whole body freeze, but a sharp look from Mr. Scant was enough to spur me into action.

I climbed uneasily down onto the dark cobble-stones of the alley. Shiny and slippery—the only time London doesn't give the impression that the rain has just stopped is when it is actually raining.

"Are we near Nelson's Column?" I asked. I knew that if we were near the National Portrait Gallery, Trafalgar Square must have been nearby. The real meaning of my question was, "Can we go and see it afterwards?" but without being so vulgar as to actually ask.

"We are," said Mr. Scant, unloading the painting, "but we are making haste."

Make haste we did—deeper into the alley. At first this confused me, but if you want to break into a museum, marching up to the front door probably isn't prudent. The scarred coachman lit a cigarette and watched us set forth into the gloom, then turned away indifferently.

"So is this near the back of the Portrait Gallery?" I asked. "That must mean we're near that new statue they made of Mr. Irving. Maybe we could sneak a look before they unveil it?"

"For the love of Pete, be quiet," Mr. Scant growled. His rudeness shocked me into silence, but what he did next would have struck me dumb in any case: from under his cloak he drew out the terrible claw and pulled it onto his right hand. Up close, the claw really was an eerie sight, with a multitude of little parts shifting and whirring with each move- ment, intricate as the innards of Father's automaton clocks. Mr. Scant knelt over a hatch in the shadows I hadn't even noticed and violently plunged one blade down into it. A moment later, we heard the sound of metal hitting the ground far below us—the padlock Mr. Scant must have cut through. Mr. Scant winced at the sound, faint though it was. Then, with some effort, he pulled the hatch open.

I wanted to ask if we were really going down into the darkness, but I hadn't quite rediscovered my voice. Luckily, there was no need, because Mr. Scant could read my expression. "Yes, this is our way into the museum, Master Oliver," he said, lashing the covered painting to his back. "No other entrance is available to us. Now, once we are inside, you must do exactly as I tell you, questioning nothing. Do we have an understanding?"

I nodded.

"Your word, please."

I thought about what he might do if I refused. "You have my word of honor. On my family name."

"Then climb down."

I looked nervously at the opening into the under-world. I could just make out the top of a ladder. "I have to go first?"

"I had your *word*."

"Once we're inside, you said. We're not inside yet."

Mr. Scant's lips pressed together. I found myself looking at those sharp, sharp blades. "No," he said, after a time. "We are not. I ask you to go first not because you are better equipped to face some great danger below, but because the hatch behind us is too heavy for you to close."

That was that. I gingerly got to the ground, and, trying not to get any dirt on my nice warm Norfolk jacket, maneuvered myself into the abyss. It crossed my mind that this might all be part of the Claw's plot to make me climb into my own grave, but why tie a painting to his back and have a man drive us to London for that? Taking what comfort I could from the thought, I began my descent.

I had no inkling of how many rungs there were to this ladder, and soon I couldn't even see the ones in front of my eyes. I remembered a story Father had once told Mother over dinner to scare her, something he liked to do. The story was about a fellow by the name of Mr. William Walker, who spent his days adding concrete to the foundations of Winchester Cathedral to stop it from falling down. But thick, muddy water surrounded the foundations, so Mr. William Walker had to put on diving gear and go about shoring up the foundations in complete darkness, underwater. One day he would finish the task, but he had been at it for years now, with no end in sight. He spent every day in that terrible void—deaf, blind, and alone. If Mr. Walker could hold his nerve through that, I ought be able endure this. This made me feel a little braver, until I remembered my descent was probably going to be the easiest part of the undertaking.

Eventually, my foot touched solid ground and I gratefully stepped down. A rush of air passed my face, which suggested Mr. Scant had let himself drop. A second later, I felt his hands grip my shoulder. Then came his voice: "Absolute silence from now on."

In the darkness, my footfalls sounded louder than a whole army on the march, while Mr. Scant may as well have been floating. Occasionally he would pull me one way or another, presumably to get around an obstacle I couldn't see, until finally I noticed a sliver of light ahead. As we approached, I could discern another ladder. This time, we climbed, and I followed after Mr. Scant. Before I was halfway to the top, he had pushed open the hatch overhead, and when I reached the final rung, he pulled me out of the earth and back into the night.

We were in a small courtyard. To our left stood a little black doorway. Mr. Scant ushered me toward it and then nodded downward. There, behind the boot-scraper, I saw a tiny little grate with a ceramic covering, which Mr. Scant stooped to prize away. The hole was hardly big enough for a shoe box; knowing what Mr. Scant intended, I started to shake my head.

"Arms in first, Master Oliver. When your shoulders are through, the rest is simple. When you're inside, *quietly* unlock the door."

"Don't tell me this is the only reason you brought me! For *this*!" I hissed.

"Of course not, Master Oliver. This way is simply the quickest way and least destructive, and I would have you remember your promise."

I did as I was told. Maneuvering around the boot-scraper proved as difficult as expected: I had to lie flat on my back and be pushed through the hole by Mr. Scant. But he hadn't been wrong—once

I wriggled my shoulders through, pulling myself inside was easy. And just like that, I had broken into my first building.

The first storage alcove of my first building, anyway. All around stood buckets and brooms—and a couple of greatcoats hung from pegs. At the sight of those, I nearly dove back through the hole, until I realized they were empty. With only a plank of wood barring the door from the inside, I soon had it open.

"Good lad," whispered Mr. Scant, stepping inside and crossing straight to the inner door. It was unlocked, so we continued through a service corridor, soon coming to another, much larger door, distinguished by more ostentatious brickwork—the entrance to the museum proper. Mr. Scant knelt to peer through the keyhole, then drew back.

"One man," he whispered. "Seated. Bored and inattentive. Here." The fingers of Mr. Scant's clawless hand pressed a stone into my palm, and I could feel the boniness of his fingers through his glove. "Aim for the little hole over the door. When I say so, throw the stone through. No need to aim for anything in particular, but be sure it goes through. Understood?"

"Understood."

"Stand close so you can be sure."

"I'm a good thrower," I said. "I'm nearly the best bowler in our form."

Mr. Scant patted me on the back, then turned his attention back to the keyhole. With one of his claws in the top part and a thin piece of metal at the bottom, he began to pick the lock, in silence as usual. Seconds later, he looked back to me and mouthed, "Now."

I tossed the pebble through the little hole. My aim was perfect, and I couldn't help a small feeling of jubilation. A second later, Mr. Scant shoved his way through the door. The guard had seen the stone drop and reached for his lamp, getting as far as "What the bl—?" before Mr. Scant was upon him.

Mr. Scant did not stab the man, as I feared he might, but what ensued was almost as distressing. With his clawed hand, Mr. Scant covered the guard's mouth, then wrapped his other arm around the man's neck to stop his breathing. Minutes must have passed before the guard stopped stamping his foot and finally went limp, and then even longer before Mr. Scant let him breathe again. "It takes longer than you might think," he whispered. "There is always the chance, when they first go still, that they are just pretending. Strangulation has its risks, but a blow to the head will too often kill a man. That is something I want to avoid where possible. Let's hope tonight it will not be necessary."

Stepping over the guard's prone figure, I was struck anew by the fact that this was no dream, and certainly no game. I had no reason to trust Mr. Scant, and no sane reason to be here with him. And yet in truth I had been oddly eager to accompany the madman, in hopes of learning more about why he had done all that he had done. Was mere curiosity really a good enough reason to risk my life?

I didn't have an answer, but it was too late to run away now.

Pressing on through the shadows, we soon came upon guards on patrol, each with a little electric torch of his own. Following Mr. Scant's signals, slipping by them was simple. I could see that none of them had been expecting an intruder, not *really*. Some five minutes into our infiltration, Mr. Scant stopped to listen, then pushed me toward a large alcove, helping me to climb up before following. We hid behind a statue as two guards passed us by, chattering about their darts club. Mr. Scant had been right: they had not even thought to look upwards.

As we pressed on through the galleries, stern-faced monarchs and ministers of the past watched us from their places on the walls. Many of the paintings were so large I felt glad the stolen one was small enough to carry. To reach the spot where the painting had originally hung, we had to pass through a large archway in the center of one of the larger galleries. Predictably, more guards were stationed in that archway than anywhere else. Mr. Scant paused at the doorway to the large gallery, then silently climbed all the way up to the picture rail before making his way, spider-like, to the arch. There, he could peer in from above, right over the heads of the guards.

"Too many," he whispered when he came back. "We'll need a distraction. A lot of noise. It's important that you stay here—go behind that bust. Even when you hear the noise, stay put, understand? When you see me go in, wait until you're sure I have their attention, then run in fast as you can and hide under the benches in the middle. You will see a piece of rope. Pull it, hard as you can. Do we have an understanding?"

"Pull the rope. Yes."

After he nodded and disappeared into the darkness, I took my position behind the bust of some lord or admiral or Lord High Admiral. For a few long minutes, I was alone. But then the noise began. I heard crashes and bangs, distant at first. Then came the yells. As they grew louder, one of the guards inside the room ordered some others to go and investigate, and I peered around the Lord High Admiral's ear to see three or four men leave the gallery. More shouts came, followed by two very loud crashes from two different directions at once—and then Mr. Scant landed right beside me.

"Be ready," growled the old man. "Head to the archway now."

When I looked back to nod, Mr. Scant was gone. After a moment to ready myself, I dashed over to the gallery entrance, just in time to hear a cry from inside. Reaching the archway, I saw Mr. Scant running along the walls, high up above the guards, holding onto the picture rail with his gloved left hand. Something he had dropped began filling the air with smoke, and Mr. Scant was cutting down pictures as he made his way around the room, putting the guards in disarray. Taking my chance, I ran inside— to see one particularly hirsute guard bellowing in outrage and producing a revolver. Mr. Scant spotted him and leapt down, drawing away the cloth that had covered the painting and wrapping it around the man's arm—then shoulder, then head. That made it easy for Mr. Scant to trip the man, who crashed to the ground before he could so much as cock the hammer of his gun.

I slid under the circle of benches in the middle of the room. All around, the confused guards were yelling. One lunged for Mr. Scant, but he jumped back and, in a flash, had climbed back up to the picture rail. Another two guards were hurrying to untangle the bearded man—presumably the one in charge—but Mr. Scant ignored them, instead making his way to where two empty picture hooks hung from the rail at the end of long wires. With the precision of a watchmaker placing cogs, he held the painting at the end of his claws and restored it to its place. From my hiding place, all I could do was gape.

I had expected the stolen painting to be a well-known masterpiece, but I had never seen this picture before. Rather than depicting some great king or famous explorer, it portrayed a rather wimpy-looking man. He was bald but for the very back of his head, where his hair was long and straggly, and he wore a suit of armor that had clearly never seen combat. He looked so ridiculous that I almost laughed. Then Mr. Scant roared, "The rope!" and I remembered myself.

Casting about in the darkness, I found the rope and pulled with all my strength. It went taut for a moment, and after a little popping sound, more smoke began to appear. Then the rope was wrested from my grip, and seeing two men fall, I realized Mr. Scant had arranged this trap not only to release more smoke but to act as a tripwire. A kind of wildness came over me: if Mr. Scant wanted people tripped, I could do it again. But before I could pull the rope tight again, a large, hairy hand came out of the smoke, grabbing my ankle.

Mr. Scant appeared over my head, precipitating himself toward the owner of the hand, and I saw a flash of metal. How strange for the awful sight of the claw to be a comfort now. From inside the circle of benches, I was unable to follow everything, but a moment later came a sound like someone beating a carpet very, very hard, and the hand gripping me went limp. I barely had time to rub the sore spot on my ankle before Mr. Scant's claw dipped down to pluck me by the collar. As if his claw were the beak of a mother bird, Mr. Scant lifted me into the air and placed me on his back.

I was on the small side for my age—not the smallest in my form, mind—but the ease with which the old man could run while bearing my weight still surprised me. Mr. Scant was wiry, but he felt solid as iron.

The bearded man was barking orders like a mad dog, but Mr. Scant dashed away so fast that the distance between us and the guards already seemed insurmountable. Nonetheless, I thought it would be wise to cover my face with my hands and peer out between my fingers, to protect my identity. The bearded man had lost his revolver but he brandished a little cosh in his fist, waving it in the air as he yelled, "Close every exit! He won't get away!"

Mr. Scant ran on, showing no sign of fatigue, and every time we encountered somebody, or even a group of somebodies, he had an answer. Some he knocked down. Some were so startled as to fall over on their own. Once, he cut a length of rope with his claw, which dropped wooden chairs on a group waiting for us, another trap I could hardly believe he had prepared in the few minutes we had been separated. He cut not a single person with the claw, but relied on speed—and sometimes elbows or fists.

Eventually, we stopped under a large balcony. Mr. Scant looked all around, and concluding we were alone, whispered, "Hold on *tight*." As he raised his claw, a mechanism within whirred, and with a jolt, the tip of one claw flew upwards. A cord trailed behind the blade, about as thick as a bootlace, and when the blade fixed on something above us, Mr. Scant cut the line with another of his claws. And then he began to climb the slender cord. I was still on his back, yet we ascended at a speed that would have impressed even our school's games master Mr. Prigg, who loved climbing ropes almost as much as he loved watching children fail to do so. The cord looked far too thin, and I was terrified the claw would slice right through it, but in moments we were up on the balcony, and Mr. Scant was winding the cord in again.

The sounds of the search continued below us. "We disappeared upwards," I whispered, delighted, but Mr. Scant shot me such a terrifying look that I bowed my head. The claw tip he'd launched had opened up like a parasol, six small metal hooks pointing outward, and anchored itself behind a baluster. Mr. Scant collapsed the hooks before reattaching the claw with a click.

When all was quiet, Mr. Scant led me to a window. Upon opening it and peering down at the road below, he once again seized me and hefted me onto his shoulder.

"Some warning would be——" I began, but that was as far as I got before he mounted the windowsill and then took to the night air. All breath left me when he jumped. I fancied that I caught a glimpse of Nelson's column, with a poacher's moon hanging in the sky behind it, before we plummeted. But it may have been a chimney stack.

I had fallen before—from trees, from my bed. I even fell off the stage once, in the Nativity Play Incident of 1903 of which we do not speak. But this was the first time I felt the suffocation of true falling, when the stomach decides to investigate what interesting things happen in the skull.

We landed on something soft, and after checking that my limbs were still attached, I looked around to see the canvas roof of the old growler carriage that had brought us to London, now quite crumpled beneath us. The driver with the scarred face regarded us, wholly unimpressed. Mr. Scant went to speak a few words to him while I sat in the indentation we had made on the roof. Then, as simply as that, and quite before I was ready, we were on the move.

Mr. Scant helped me clamber off the roof and into the carriage, and then weathered the assault of my words, which I simply couldn't stop. "What was that? We jumped off the roof! How can we . . . What was the . . . ? That was the most terrifying thing I've done in my whole life!" There was no helping it; a dam had burst. "And we disappeared upwards, just like you said! We did! And then downwards! Oh, if Father could only have seen! That man had a revolver! What if he had shot us?"

"That bulldog? Only for show, I assure you, Master Oliver," said Mr. Scant, impossibly calm. "Putting a hole through one of the paintings is not something one in that man's position would risk. The directors of the National Portrait Gallery are notoriously more concerned about their floors than their patrons. He would not have dared shoot us, I think, without a mop nearby for our blood."

"Urgh," I said. But the chilling thought didn't keep me quiet for long. "You really put the painting back, though! So, what, is this what you do? You return stolen things to their owners, like a—"

"Enough, Master Oliver. There will be time for

talk later. You must sleep. There will not be much opportunity for it once we are home."

"I couldn't possibly sleep after—"

"You can, and you will."

Cold-eyed, Mr. Scant opened the carriage door and swung himself out to sit with the scarred man in the driving seat. I was left alone with the strange sight of the severely dented roof—and with my thoughts. The last one I had before I fell asleep concerned how entirely impossible it would be for me to sleep.

V

A Day without Ice

The first thing I registered when Mr. Scant woke me was the biting cold. With its roof damaged, the growler wasn't keeping the night air out, so the chill had crept into my bones while I slept. I looked out of the window to see we'd reached Father's driveway, and all at once I remembered everything I had just lived through. Even so, I no longer felt sleep was impossible. In fact, I wanted little else.

"We must be silent," said Mr. Scant, who carried a small sack over his shoulder, presumably with the claw inside. I nodded.

Crossing the lawn to avoid the gravel path, we entered through the kitchens. It was the first time I had ever seen them so still: they were never quiet for a moment while Mrs. George was awake. Mr. Scant escorted me through the house and up to my room, where my bedclothes were still laid out. I yawned as I picked them up, and Mr. Scant bowed. "Well, then, Master Oliver," he said, which was his way of saying goodnight.

"Mr. Scant?" I said.

"Master Oliver?"

"I'm sorry I forgot to pull the rope."

"One small element of a successful operation."

"I should have felt awful if I made a mess of the whole thing," I admitted, struggling to unbutton my jacket with fingers that seemed twice as large as usual. I wanted a nice long bath, but not nearly as much as I wanted a nice long sleep.

"That was never a possibility," Mr. Scant said.

"Funny that your . . . rivals chose that painting out of all the masterpieces they could have taken. I thought it would be a painting of Mr. Shakespeare or Mr. Purcell, someone like that. Not that funny little bald man. Who was he?"

"The painting is quite valuable; it was painted by Sir Anthony van Dyck, of whom I am sure you are aware. The subject was one Sir Kenelm Digby. He was the son of one of the conspirators in the Guy Fawkes plot, as well as an eminent scientist and, for a time, a pirate of sorts."

"Really? That funny little chap?"

"Perhaps that will show you not to judge by appearances. Yes, that funny little chap. My . . . adversaries stole the portrait not for Sir Digby's fame, though it was great in his day, but for his reputation as a worker of magic. He was said to have the power to take a blade that injured a man, and upon applying a few grains of a magic powder to the weapon, heal the wounded party."

"Was it true?"

"I think not, Master Oliver, but the idea captivated a great many minds at the time—and captivates them still today. Now, I must begin my preparations for your father's breakfast and morning ablutions. You must sleep."

With that, he gave his usual smart bow and withdrew. My plump collection of pillows had done without me all night long, and now it greeted me eagerly as I finished changing and hopped into bed. I allowed myself a chuckle as I settled in. Such incredible things I had seen! Nobody in my school could boast the same. Nobody I had ever met, most likely—save Mr. Scant himself.

Of course, I still had an avalanche of questions. How did Mr. Scant know the painting was stolen, and who had done the deed, if not him? Was there another Claw, and who was the man he had been fighting on the fateful night of my discovery? But soon my thoughts were a blur of funny bald men making magical tinctures on pirate ships, and I dropped into a dream. And as is the usual way of dreams, mine had nothing to do with my exploits with Mr. Scant or with Sir Kenelm Digby. Rather, my dream concerned Peter Clephane trying to convince me to buy a new kind of apple—with wings, costing 2d.

When Penny woke me, I felt restored, which came as quite a surprise. Apparently Mr. Scant had put it about that I had been ill and coughing in the night, and so Penny allowed me to sleep later than usual and even to miss breakfast. After washing, I dressed in the comfortable Saturday clothes Penny had laid out for me, including a navy blue neckerchief and matching long trousers. Until I finished prep school, I was condemned to wear short trousers on school days, and my Sunday best usually had to be breeches, so long trousers were something of a Saturday treat.

I went downstairs in time to see Mr. Scant step out of the drawing room with the day's paper on a tray, so hurried over to ask if there was anything in it of particular interest.

"For you, I think not, Master Oliver," said Mr. Scant. He was back to being deferential. I could hardly believe this was the same man who had jumped off a roof with me on his back only hours earlier. "This is the early edition, of course," he added. "Your mother will be pleased to see you are in good health. She is in her rooms with Mrs. Winton at present, but asked to be told when you had risen. I will let her know you will wait for her in the music room. Or would you prefer the long gallery?"

"Long gallery please, Mr. Scant," I said, enjoying this game of pretense. I remained terrified of Mr. Scant and a long way from understanding the true nature of the Ruminating Claw, but when you have jumped out of a window with someone, a strange kind of camaraderie develops.

"I am told no rain is expected after lunch. Your father is home all day but not to be disturbed, so perhaps you ought to play outside?"

This was a very strange request to hear from him, but I understood. "I'll tell Mother I might meet with my friends."

"A splendid idea."

Mother and I had a custom if she found me lying on the settee in the long gallery: she would gently lift my head and lay it on her lap. Then she would sing to herself as she played with my hair, or talk softly with her maid, Mrs. Winton. Having my head stroked made me feel a tad babyish, but it was a pleasant sensation—and if I avoided it, Mother would ask me why. So while I allowed her to part my hair this way and that, she asked the usual things: about my studies, if I still hoped to join the school rugby team, whether I'd learned any new Bible passages. It was easy to mention I might meet my friends later on, and she had no objections. Then something else crossed my mind.

"Mother?" I said.

"Mmm?"

"Does Father think I'm a coward?"

Mother didn't take much time to think about this. "Of course not, my darling," she cooed, which I was sure she would have said no matter what she really thought.

I ended up dozing for a little while, there on her lap, which she seemed to enjoy. Afterward, wrapped up against the afternoon cold but not knowing what else to expect, I wandered into the garden. The grounds were modest. Only one-and-a-half acres, a lone flowerpot when compared with the family gardens of the likes of Skipper Percival, the rugby captain—his had stables and everything. Even so, we had trees to hide behind and bushes to slip between. Behind one tree I found Mr. Scant, and although I had been looking for him, his sudden appearance gave me a start.

"Still afraid of me?" he asked, as I clutched a hand to my chest.

"Wouldn't you be?"

"Yes, I suppose I would. Now, I have somewhere we can talk. From this day forth, matters of importance are to be discussed there and only there. This way."

Taking care to keep out of sight of the house, Mr. Scant led me to the little grass bank behind the gardener's shed.

"The coal bunker?" I said.

"The Ice House," said Mr. Scant.

"We don't have an ice house," I said, with a little laugh. The idea was silly. "Only big country estates have ice houses."

"And yet . . ." Mr. Scant said. He took out a long, silver key and, as if at random, pushed it into a patch of grass. Stranger still, he then grasped a thin iron ring I hadn't been able to see and opened up the ground. The mound I had thought to be nothing but a pile of earth, designed to hide the coal bunker from the house, was in fact part of a solid structure, complete with a small wooden doorway. "A manor once stood on these grounds, and this was built for it many years ago," said Mr. Scant. "It has since been forgotten, but the structure is easily found. With improvements to the brickwork, it became fit for my purposes."

"You have a secret lair," I said. "I'm not quite sure I believe this."

"In you pop," said Mr. Scant, his voice so flat that the whimsical choice of words did not seem peculiar.

In I popped. A narrow passage inside led to a larger, decidedly chilly space. I heard a kind of mechanical roar, and then light began to fill the ice house. I had heard that sound before, in Father's factories: Mr. Scant had an electric generator.

More of a shock than the light was what it revealed: a cavernous space the shape of a vast bell. The lair of the Ruminating Claw. A number of wooden platforms lined its periphery, with a sturdy framework underneath supporting a long staircase.

Each platform housed a little workshop of sorts: I saw various machines for cutting wood or sharpening metal, apparatus for mixing chemicals, and a desk half-buried beneath research materials.

"Well then, Master Oliver," Mr. Scant said. "Come in and settle down. There is a comfortable armchair and a stove for tea below. The burner will warm the place up a little."

"Only a little?" I said, letting my teeth chatter in a demonstrative sort of a way.

"Only a little. I am not a man who much needs excess warmth."

"Surprising," I said. "If ever they write about your exploits, I'll be sure to make them include that revelation. Otherwise, people might assume you love coziness and sunshine."

"Say what you like here, Master Oliver, but please, no jokes about documenting my exploits. If anyone should ever write of my misdeeds, I would have your assurance that it will be without any assistance from you."

I had been forgetting myself after the night's adventure, but seeing the severity of Mr. Scant's expression, I remembered that he was not a man I ever ought to tease.

"I'm sorry."

"Your assurance."

"I swear I'll never tell a soul. On the honor of my family."

"Splendid." He had a way of speaking that joyful word that made it shrivel up into "vaguely acceptable."

At the bottom of all the rickety wooden stairs sat a rather battered armchair. I amused myself with the thought of Mr. Scant wrestling it down the steps of the lair, but didn't dare let my amusement show on my face. Alongside the burner, Mr. Scant had installed an equally sorry-looking rocking chair, with its varnish peeling and most of the front of the left rocker missing. It was into this that Mr. Scant settled, then began to rock softly. The way he looked at me put me in mind of when I had seen a huge bear scratching his back on a tree at the zoo—his expression challenged me, *dared* me to laugh.

I suspected that Mr. Scant was waiting for me to talk, so I cleared my throat. "So, ah . . . you never really explained about the painting. You . . . didn't steal it?"

"I was not the one who took it from the National Portrait Gallery, no."

"So . . . you're not the master criminal, then."

"I am not responsible for the crimes pinned on the Ruminating Claw, as the press likes to call me. I have never engaged in the theft of an item that was not already stolen property."

"So who is the original thief?"

"It will have been someone acting in collaboration with my brother."

"Your brother?"

"Indeed. My younger brother, Reginald."

"Reginald Scant." It struck me that I didn't know Mr. Scant's given name. "Reginald and . . . ?"

Mr. Scant ignored me, rising to prepare some tea.

"In fact, he goes by the legal name of Reginald *Gaunt*. While on the brink of bankruptcy, he didn't want the family name to appear in reports that could be considered disgraceful, so he changed it. Later in life, he deemed it wise to keep the name, something that has made life easier for me."

"It sounds complicated."

"Reginald and I were very close when we were young," said Mr. Scant, in a tone that suggested I should get comfortable because there was much to be said. "We were born into a family that, while not wealthy, was full of love and ambition. My father was a seafaring man. We saw little of him, but the times he came home were some of the happiest I have ever known. Our family trips to see the construction of the greatest ships of the age showed me the wondrous things that are possible when great minds work together.

"As children, Reginald and I took interest in the sciences. I gravitated toward the mechanical, and he toward the chemical. We were eager to learn all we could, and my mother supported us in every way she knew. She sold her jewels and our grandmother's silks for our books and rudimentary equipment. My father's navy service gave us entry to a school that our station in life would not otherwise have allowed, and after our father died in battle, kind souls who felt a sense of obligation ensured Reginald and I stayed there until we were young men."

"I'm sorry to hear that."

"You were expecting my parents to be alive and well?" Mr. Scant turned away, busying himself with the stove and kettle. "As Reginald and I sought to find our way in the world, science remained our shared passion. After a brief military service, I mostly worked in printing and photography, helping some very clever men improve the processes they had invented, while my brother pursued the refinement of combustible fuels. Well, he was the more successful of the two of us—he had rather a good idea for improving efficiency in the refinement of crude oil, and I helped him design a chamber to put his theory into practice. We never did anything so fine as when we worked together."

"You must have got on well. I'd like to have a brother like that myself."

"It was a happy time. But by this stage, Reggie had become quite the popular man about town, and the ability to keep secrets was a talent he never possessed, especially not after working a little too eagerly with his ethanol supply. Though the industrialists who had licensed Reginald's machine already stood to make a considerable amount of money, they realized they would receive significantly more if his patents were transferred to the company. Though he was married by then, Reginald enjoyed boasting to women of everything he had achieved. One night, a young lady invited Reggie to join him for a ride in a hackney carriage. Once inside, he discovered some other passengers were also along for the ride. I don't know what was said to him in that carriage, but he handed over his invention, his patents . . . soon, his home followed. He lost everything. Even the good-will of our mother."

"Why?"

"Ah, they were clever, the enemies he made, and numerous."

By then, the tea was ready. Mr. Scant brought over his tea set—a surprisingly dainty one, with a soft, bluebell design—and settled back into his rocking chair. He knew how I liked my tea—still with two sugars, despite Mother's disapproval. Since Mr. Scant took no sugar, I wondered if he had brought some down especially for me. As I blew the tea to cool it down, Mr. Scant drank steadily from his cup, then went on.

"There is a group of rich men and women called the Woodhouselee Society, named for a clever Scotsman who argued that no true democracy exists while leaders can be corrupted—that electing a leader means giving up freedom. This society seeks not to reform this system but to exploit it. The members believe that a corrupt democracy, run by the elite, is inevitable, and so they take pains to *be* that elite. They are more interested in political control than other, similar fraternities . . . and believe that with enough money and influence, they will be able to control the Empire no matter who governs."

"And they went after your brother?"

"The industrialists who funded his research were Woodhouselee members. It was not hard for them to discover Reggie's weakness for drink—almost everybody knew it at the time. Well, I say that, but while I knew it, Reggie's wife, Winifred, knew it, and all of his enemies knew it—our mother did not. So when Reggie began to resist the advances of the Society, breaking his spirit was as simple as letting him slip into a drunken rage and then introducing our mother to the scene. She was a hard woman, our mother, as you might surmise. Not one to hide her disappointment. Reggie, for his part, was not quite sensible with so much drink in him, and the scar he gave his own mother, right across her mouth, made him a stranger to her to her deathbed. She called for him there, but by then, it was beyond my power to fetch him."

The best I could think of was, "That's so sad."

Mr. Scant drank deeply from his cup. "Now, Reggie lost everything, but that was by no means the end of his suffering. People like the ones who have their talons in him, they don't let go. His mind remained of use to them. They made sure he remained in their debt. Heavily in debt. Tens of thousands of pounds, if you can imagine it. Reggie had a wife to protect, and later a child, a beautiful little girl, Elspeth. This was before you were born—Ellie must be fifteen or sixteen years old now. And my brother had already been the Society's puppet some ten years by the time she was born. All this time, Reggie has done the only thing he can: *everything* those villains demand. Little by little, he imagines, he will repay them." Mr. Scant wiped a hand down his face, and though his eyes were dry, he looked for a moment like a much older man than he was.

"How could he ever repay that much?"

"How indeed? Years have passed since the society took his patents, with his debts barely reduced. But in recent months, things have changed. Reggie has been working like a slave, but there is only so much ingenuity in one man, and now he is old and slow. At some point in the last year or so, someone proposed a way to make better use of his talents."

"To do with the . . . thieving?"

"Indeed. You see, as with most gatherings of rich, bored men and women, the Woodhouselee Society has a great interest in the mystical. Its members make a great study of alchemy and believe that certain figures belonged to a hidden order controlling the world—Sir Kenelm Digby, Sir Isaac Newton, Sir Francis Bacon, to name a few. A common fancy amongst men with too much money but no real influence. Not only do they believe occult societies have occupied the position of power and influence they covet, they believe that if they do not have knowledge of magical objects, others who do will supplant them."

"So they believe in magic?"

"Whether they believe in it is largely irrelevant. If there is any possibility at all they will lose power and influence because others have magic and they do not, why risk losing out? So the Society has recruited specialists in artworks connected to magic and alchemy, and at their recommendation, began to steal them. Of course, none of the items had any magical effects. At first, the Woodhouselee men meant to keep the stolen items as trophies, but they soon realized far more profit was to be made from selling them—to buyers in the far Orient, curious about the old magic of Europe. You see, a certain confidence trickster going by the name of Lord Boleskine has established a trade there in supposedly magical items."

"And your brother steals them?"

"No. My brother would not be of any use to his captors in that regard. The two of us have lived very different lives. But he remains a highly gifted chemist. Some would call him a genius. The Society has enlisted that genius in the making of forgeries. Why sell one painting when you can sell three counterfeits, or thirty, with the pigments recreated to perfection? Why take a jewel and risk being hounded for the rest of your days when you can replace it with a copy so convincing that nobody ever investigates?"

"So why not just make perfect copies and sell those, then say the one in the galleries is the fake?"

"A salient question, Master Oliver. There are two reasons. Firstly, gifted as Reggie is, he almost always requires the original to make a convincing replica—a process that is not always an overnight affair. Secondly, the Woodhouselee Society would be challenged to convince its buyers a switch had been made in complete secrecy: reports of the thefts are useful for persuading buyers they are purchasing the true original. Reginald's part in all this makes him worth keeping alive, and I am told his work is now making a genuine difference to his debts. But naturally, I will not allow it."

"Because in the end he'll be caught?"

"Not so much that as for my mother's sake. She died still grieving that her son had fallen to a life of crime and violence: I will not allow that to become reality."

"So you became the criminal instead?"

Mr. Scant gave me such a sharp look that for a moment I worried I had gone too far.

"There are crimes and there are crimes. Trespass, yes. Offenses against the person . . . on occasion, though it's not something I relish. Mother would have seen the necessity. It is another matter to provide direct support to criminals hoping to undermine the entire government. So I took the thieves' idea of returning the items after they were stolen, but I ensure this happens before they can reach Reggie's laboratory."

"Won't they punish your brother if it keeps going wrong?"

"My brother is but one cog in a machine. If anything, he is the last one they ought to suspect, since the goods never reach his hands."

I took a sip of my tea while I tried to understand all this. As usual, Mr. Scant's Darjeeling was brewed perfectly. One thing continued to bother me. "But . . . if you're stopping him from doing this forgery, doesn't that mean his debt will never be repaid?"

Mr. Scant let out a breath. "Yes. He may even resent me for it. But I would sooner bear his scorn than let him become something he emphatically is not—a true criminal."

"Why doesn't he run away?"

"He is watched. His family too. The Wood-houselee Society has arranged a good life for Reginald's daughter, Elspeth, which placates him better than any opium pipe. She has a place at a superlative school in France—under the Society's watch, as Reginald well knows. Young Elspeth is clever but troubled. She has a powerful gift for mathematics . . . but finds other people more of a puzzle. When they took her away, Reggie grew lazy and compliant. Which leaves me to right his wrongs. Or, more precisely, to stop them from ever happening."

"But this can't go on forever, surely? Whoever does the stealing in the first place, they're going to want to . . . to get you. If you're standing in their way, they'll set a trap!"

"Yes. Yes, I'm afraid that can't be denied. Which is how we arrive at the man you saw me subdue in the night, an agent of the Woodhouselee Society. My greatest blunder—I noticed him following me and took flight. When he was able to track me even to the roof of this building, I realized he had to be dealt with. I subdued the man, but as I was carrying him down through the house, he displayed the ability to dislocate his joints and free himself from his restraints. Remarkable, really. We fought for a second time, which was where you spotted me. He is now a very long way away, and not likely to betray any secrets—even if he has them."

"You didn't do him in?"

The sneer on Mr. Scant's lips suggested he didn't appreciate the question. "No. No, I did not 'do him in.' I saw no need. I simply sent him on a long voyage to Shanghai."

"In China?"

"The only Shanghai of which I am aware. The Woodhouselee Society wants to hawk its goods there, so I thought I should send him to negotiate in person."

"Gosh. China. I've never been further than Edinburgh. I don't suppose I'll ever get so far from home. I can't imagine being stuck in a crate all that time . . ."

"Who said anything about a crate?" Mr. Scant said. "Though a crate *was* involved, as it happens."

"What would have happened if he had run away instead of fighting you?"

"I may be getting old, Master Oliver, but I could still easily catch up to the likes of him, and he knew it. On the other hand, a few years ago, I would have noticed him regain consciousness instantaneously. A sign of age, I fear."

I gave a little smile. "Are you losing your touch?"

Mr. Scant did not smile back. That is to say, he carried on not smiling. But he attained an even more profound level of frostiness, probably a new depth for mankind. "That may very well be the case," he said. "I would not have been so careless even three years ago. And if I must still wage this little war of mine three years from now . . . who can say if I will still be capable? One mistake can mean incarceration, disgrace, or worse."

"I suppose so."

"That, of course, is where you come in, Master Oliver."

"Where I . . . ?"

"I am not certain it is possible—or wise. But the reason I asked you to accompany me, and the reason I am now taking you into my confidence, is the increasing likelihood that I will need assistance."

I swallowed. "Do you mean . . . something like an apprentice?"

"You could call it that."

"How would we even begin?"

"We begin," said Mr. Scant, "with your mind."

VI
The Valkyrie

My new life began, disappointingly, with study.

The most important thing, Mr. Scant told me, was to understand the world and how it worked. To look at things differently, always with a goal in mind. And with his guidance, I saw how the dull equations in school could be the keys to understanding one of Mr. Scant's machines, or how Mr. Ibberts's desert-dry history lectures were full of clues to what drove rich and powerful men. Mr. Scant would ask me to learn about a particular sculptor or painter, and if Father didn't have a book about him, I'd find one in the school library during break.

My friends were a bit nonplussed by this new behavior. Chudley even tutted at me, saying he thought I cared more about books than rugger these days. But I swatted him about the head and made a point of proving him wrong during the next practice, because Mr. Scant would surely want me to improve my strength and stamina next. It could do no harm to get a head start.

To my surprise, Mr. Scant was displeased when I told him about the encounter. "Why strike him?" he asked.

"He didn't mind. We're friends. We've been friends since we were five years old and he taught me the secret to stopping Big-Jaw Watts in the year above from stealing my lunch was to stomp on his toes. We're still friends."

"When we spoke about your mind, that did not mean only *knowledge*. Understanding the contents of books is well and good, but understanding people is vastly more important. You must be able to perceive what others want from you and then please them. To make them enjoy your presence. Then, you can learn from them—and they will know if you are insincere. I advise you to practice."

"So I should make people like me the way they like you?"

"Don't try my patience, Master Oliver."

I walked away from him muttering, but didn't dare say anything more. Now that I no longer suspected that he was on the brink of murdering me, I had relaxed around Mr. Scant, but the possibility remained that he could decide I ought to be silenced.

So I decided to heed his advice. The next day, I told Chudley I was sorry for hitting him. I even did it in front of Bert Simmons rather than waiting for a quiet moment. Chudley looked a bit confused, and I didn't blame him: nobody ever said sorry at school unless a teacher was making them. "Don't be soft," he said. "Just wanted to make sure you're not getting too big for your boots."

"Because I was reading books?"

"No—because you . . . I dunno, you started looking at us funny, is all. All smug."

"Well, I . . . That wasn't my intention. And I shouldn't have hit you."

"Barely noticed it. What, should I cry every time the wind makes a weed brush against me?"

I laughed. "Weed, is it? And who won last time we arm-wrestled?"

"Er, if I recall correctly, that was you *and* Richards *and* Macclesfield all at once."

"Still counts."

"It really doesn't!"

Going back to normal was as simple as that.

To my surprise, the newspapers made little fuss about the return of the painting. After a few days, a notice deep in the *Twopence Herald* mentioned damage to the gallery, but the reporting was simple and perfunctory. Mr. Scant said that because the papers didn't understand why a thief would return a painting, they didn't know how to write the story properly and so avoided it.

Every so often I would meet Mr. Scant's eye, and a small movement of his head in the direction of the garden would let me know to meet him that evening in the Ice House. By and by I began to grow familiar with his different machines and their functions: the one for sharpening the blades of the claw, which I wasn't allowed to go near; the one for coiling rope extremely tightly; the one for making canisters that let out smoke or sticky paste. Mr. Scant had given names to most of these machines—Martha, Bessie, Henrietta—which was very like what Father did with his engines at work. What would Father have thought, I wondered, if he knew all this was going on under the surface of his property? Indeed, how much of this equipment had been quietly purloined from Father's stores? I dared not ask.

After about a week and a half of this, I received the nod after my tutoring session. I met Mr. Scant in the garden and entered the Ice House, chirping to him about the latest set of chemical elements I had committed to memory. He met this accomplishment with a hand held up for silence.

"What's wrong?" I asked, as Mr. Scant hurried down the rickety stairs.

"The time we have been preparing for is at hand," he said, meeting my eye only for a moment. "As you know, King Edward passed away earlier in the year, and His Majesty King George has not yet been crowned. For some months, preparations have been underway for his coronation."

"Right," I said. "We had a lesson with Mrs. Bell about how even if he won't be crowned until next year, the history books still say he reigned from 1910. Some of my teachers talk about the coronation so much we think they expect to get an invitation."

"Shortly after the ceremony, His Majesty the King is to travel to India. There are parts of His Highness's empire where his subjects may be confused about the power that a man from some strange foreign land holds over their lives, so a second coronation is to be held there. Now, as you may know, the crown itself must never leave this fair land. Yet His Highness is expected to wear one for this appearance abroad. To resolve this dilemma, a wholly new crown has been made, affixed with six thousand and more precious jewels."

"They stole it?"

"Ah, now, that I think would be a task beyond even our little Woodhouselees. An object worth tens of thousands of pounds and meant for the head of a king is not put on display like a mere oil painting."

"But didn't you once steal the Sword of Mercy? That's one of the Crown Jewels."

"Don't forget, the Society did the initial stealing. I did the returning. But yes, I held Curtana for a time, before I could return it. All I can say of the matter is that iron bars work well for stopping the theft of crowns. They are of less use in protecting long, thin objects."

"So you got to hold something from the Crown Jewels!"

"Only until I could be rid of the thing. In any case, stealing the new crown is simply beyond the resources of the Society. Of interest to them, and therefore to us, are the magical rituals associated with the Crown Jewels. There have been kings in this land since the times of dragon-slaying and swords in stones and suchlike, if we believe the legends. As a result, the king's advisors in such matters have taken an old book of magic—the thoroughly Christian kind, you understand—out of a secret part of the British Library, so that its spells of protection could be cast upon the crown. That is a prize our adversaries could scarcely resist."

"A book of magic?"

"A grimoire, they call it. A very old book entitled *The Grand Song of Solomon*. I mentioned before that the Woodhouselee Society associates with specialists in old magic, did I not? At least one of them is a magician secretly employed by the Palace to conduct any rituals they feel they need."

"The Royal Family believes in all this?"

"Likely not. The whole affair is probably considered part of the crown's . . . manufacturing process, if you will. But is a blessing from a magical book any stranger than the other rituals that happen at the coronation?"

"I suppose not," I said. "So they mean to steal this book?"

"Indeed. The advisors stored it at the library at St. James' Square after the ritual was completed, where it awaits return to the British Library. The Society was able give my brother access to the tome until the copy was ready, and now they have made their switch."

"So the book's already been stolen?"

"Indeed. I confess, we are late to act. This has been an unusual crime for the Society—no infiltration of a museum or gallery took place, so my source could not forewarn me. What pains Reginald went to in reproducing an entire grimoire, I cannot say. But since a member of the Society was officially charged with keeping the book, Reggie is not a criminal until the original is sold. So the sale is what we must prevent."

As Mr. Scant finished speaking, a sound startled me, sudden and strange: Mr. Scant had pulled his claw on with such force that it made a thick, clanking noise. A few moments later, I realized what this meant.

"We're going *now*?" I said.

"Any later and I risk not being able to make proper arrangements for dinner. And as you know, I take my duties seriously."

The location of the secret headquarters of Mr. Scant's enemies made squeezing in a death-defying operation before dinner surprisingly feasible.

"*Mrs. McBunty's house?*" I said, pointing to the property directly opposite ours.

"Indeed. The dear old grimalkin knows nothing of it, of course."

"And . . . they don't know you live here?"

"Of course not. That would make life extraordinarily difficult."

"Then . . . you chose to work for Father because he lived in the house opposite?"

"Where better?"

"Mr. Scant, sometimes I think you might be a lunatic."

"I am certain this isn't the first time you've thought so, Master Oliver. But the house itself is not the Wood-houselee Society's meeting place. It is simply one of several entrances. We have a long walk ahead of us."

"So what do you want me to do?"

My mission, Mr. Scant told me firmly, was to stay watchful and out of sight as we entered the tunnel under Mrs. McBunty's house. According to

Mr. Scant, the members of the Society would do far worse things than the guards in the portrait gallery if they caught me. And, he informed me with his usual ruthlessness, my being caught here would also compromise Mr. Scant's mission—whereas, in the gallery, he could have replaced the painting no matter what became of me.

"Glad to know where we stand," I said.

Though the house in question stood opposite my family's own, that did not mean it was within a stone's throw. Properties here were large, ringed by high walls meant to deter undesirables—such as Mr. Scant and myself, I supposed. But garden walls were no deterrent to the Ruminating Claw and his apprentice: Mr. Scant lifted me to the top of the McBunty residence as though I weighed no more than Father's newspaper. I dropped down behind a convenient rhododendron, Mr. Scant so close behind that he nearly landed before I did.

"I need you within arm's reach at all times," he whispered, pulling his scarf up to cover his face and supplying me with one too. As I wrapped it around my neck, he added, "But if we see the Valkyrie, run and hide immediately. Now, silence from this moment on."

The trouble with this silence, of course, was that it did not allow me to ask the very pressing question of who or what this Valkyrie might be. But Mr. Scant had already turned away and commenced creeping toward the house. To gain access, we had to scale a chestnut tree whose branches grew close to a balcony. Mr. Scant climbed as quickly as he ran, but he knew exactly when I could follow his route unaided and when I would need his help to reach a branch or a hollow in the bark. Once we were as close as we could get to the balcony while on solid footing, Mr. Scant insisted on taking me on his back again, and I felt once more the strange solidity of his frame, as though he and Mrs. George in the kitchens had done a deal with the Devil so that everything tough and dense was transferred to him, while she got all the softness. And then he jumped.

As we landed, Mr. Scant bent down so deeply that I could have sworn his knees came up past my head. Though our landing made almost no sound, it did dislodge an icicle from the edge of the balcony. Mr. Scant actually gave it a glare as he set me down.

From there, we found entry easily enough, through a pair of unlocked French windows. Mrs. McBunty had one of those funny circular reception rooms with two narrow staircases running down along the walls, like the top half of an imperial staircase. They ran around a table in the middle topped by a vase of well-kept flowers. As we descended one staircase, Mr. Scant kept a close eye on the other, while I did my best to be quiet as a mouse wearing cotton wool shoes. Fittingly, one of Mrs. McBunty's many spoilt cats watched us with hungry eyes, but the household staff was nowhere to be seen.

Halfway down the steps, I could hear Mrs. McBunty in another room. She had company—most likely her best friend, Mrs. MacIntosh.

". . . all planned out for Christmas," Mrs. McBunty was saying with satisfaction. "I shall take what my girl Daisy gave me last year and give it to Irene at the church, and I shall take what Irene gave me for my birthday and give it to Daisy's girl Juliet, and Juliet always gives me something with cats, so I shall give that to Mrs. Smith. You know she likes cats too, that one."

"And who gave you the present you're to pass off to me, then?" I heard Mrs. MacIntosh ask, and then we were out of earshot. Mr. Scant gently picked up a nearby cat and proceeded through an innocuous servants' door, which led to some stone steps very like the ones in my family's house. I wondered what Mr. Scant wanted with this cat until I realized several doors had been carefully closed to stop the house's pets from getting through. When Mr. Scant set the creature down and shooed it into the kitchen, it didn't take long for chaos to erupt. As the maids busied themselves trying to catch the creature, Mr. Scant pulled me in through the kitchen doors and we dashed behind the big table. I caught a glimpse of the cat jumping from shelf to shelf with the three kitchen maids hurrying in pursuit. After we reached the pantry, Mr. Scant revealed a trapdoor, which he pulled open, shooing me in just as he had shooed the cat.

Once we had climbed down and Mr. Scant had handed me an electric torch, he apparently decided silence was no longer necessary. "This is one of eight or nine entrances to the Society's favorite stronghold. Others run from a church or two, from the old schoolhouse, and no doubt many other places I have yet to discover."

"So nothing happens in Mrs. McBunty's house?"

"It is only an entrance. Though I suspect she is not wholly oblivious."

"Do they not think to put guards there?"

"Perhaps the maids were the guards. But these passages are envisioned more as escape routes than guarded entrances."

It was true. The tunnel led to a sentry's hut, but Mr. Scant walked up to it without a modicum of caution. As we drew close, I recognized the man posted there as the driver with the scarred face who had taken us to London. He must have been Mr. Scant's contact inside the Woodhouselee Society.

"You're late," said the scarred man, his voice as lacerated as his face. "The buyers are here."

"And the Valkyrie?" said Mr. Scant, in a voice low enough that I barely heard it.

"She's got the book. And yes, it's the real one." This earned the man a pat on the shoulder. As I passed, the scarred man's eyes followed me, and even when I lost my nerve and looked away, I could feel them on my back.

Soon, the tunnel gave way to a wide, open space. Gray winter light spilled in from a round hole above us, and I could hear running water. "Where are we?" I asked.

"A kind of water palace. You will have drunk the water at the Pantiles, of course."

"I have." The famous spring water of Tunbridge

Wells, rich with minerals, drew more visitors to the town than any other attraction, and the place to drink it was the Pantiles.

"What you may not know is that chalybeate water can be found in many other places, even within the town. This is another spring, discovered some years ago. A young entrepreneur intended to make a new attraction here, a spa of sorts. Only he decided to first jump off Beachy Head in what he claimed was a flying suit, so the project was never finished. Now it is all but forgotten—except amongst the Society, which makes good use of the grounds."

This explained the strange half-finished neo-classical design, all false pillars and empty alcoves. A number of iron grills let in the light from above, and underneath them, unpleasant brown patches of decayed leaves had piled up. This was a sad, forgotten place, and I couldn't decide what would be worse— to be buried and forgotten, or to be appropriated by a merciless criminal organization.

"This way," said Mr. Scant, and we were moving again. We descended an elegant staircase, to a level darker than the last, and after making our way down several corridors, we came to a wide, open space filled with crates and boxes gathering dust. There,

Mr. Scant stopped so abruptly that I almost walked into him. Then he grabbed me and pulled me behind one of the crates.

Before I could demand an explanation, I heard voices, speaking in a language I couldn't understand. The sounds vaguely resembled schoolyard imitations of Chinese, but I had never heard the real language spoken, so I couldn't be sure. Mr. Scant remained still as a statue, his upheld hand a clear signal to keep silent, until the speakers were almost upon us—then, faster than a rabbit bolting for its warren, he surged through the door. By the time I had stepped out, he had already dealt with two of the men, who lay groaning on the floor now. I could tell that Mr. Scant had knocked their heads together, and remembered what he had told me in the National Portrait Gallery: *a blow to the head will too often kill a man.* I tried not to think about it.

Two other men squared off against Mr. Scant with knives in their hands. I had seen numerous drawings of the Chinese on those old-fashioned plates and cabinets, but they were always merry, plump little fellows with smooth faces. These men were tall, rough, bearded, and fearsome. As one lunged forward with his blade, the other drew back and yelled something

I presumed was in his own language. *"Fee-fi!"* he yelled, almost screaming. *"Fee-fi!"*

Mr. Scant tutted in annoyance, grabbed the wrist of the man coming at him, and twisted it in such a way that the man fell to his knees, crying in pain. The old man then used his opponent's shoulder as a springboard, which sent him crashing headfirst to the floor. From there, Mr. Scant rose up into the air with his claw spreading like an eagle's talons, but rather than slash at his assailant, he swung his foot in a wide arc and caught the man on the side of the head. As Mr. Scant landed, he took a moment to make sure none of the four men were able to stand, then grabbed me by the arm.

"She will be coming for us," he said. "These men don't have the book yet, so the exchange has not been made. Now, back the way we came. We need to get away from these men before they recover; if she gets here, I won't be able to fight them all at once."

"Who is 'she'?" I tried to ask, but we were already running.

We nearly reached the staircase before a huge arm came out of the shadows to close the door ahead of us. Out stepped a huge woman, so tall that even Mr. Scant could have stood no higher than her shoulders. She was nearly as broad as she was high, almost square-shaped, but looked more muscular than obese: from where I stood half-hidden behind Mr. Scant, she appeared roughly as solid and imposing as the average town hall. The woman drew out two large meat cleavers and grinned a wicked grin. She wore a breastplate like the Valkyries from some silly opera, and over it hung a stained butcher's apron.

"Fo-fum," she said, and licked her lips. Now I understood that the Chinese man had not yelled something in another language but rather a code word to summon this beast.

"Do we dance this dance again, my dear?" Mr. Scant rumbled, pushing me back.

"Well, old man, perhaps I want to dance with a new partner," cooed the Valkyrie. I cringed as she widened her hungry eyes at me. "Pretty boy. Pretty clothes, pretty hair. Do you like dancing, boy, ha?"

"He's not yours to take. Don't you know I punish those who steal?"

"So says the famous *thief*!"

She swung her cleaver up at Mr. Scant's belly with a force that would have split him in two. Another attack forced us back down the corridor, and Mr. Scant shoved me into a side room. I hid behind one of the wooden crates inside and tried to convince my body to melt into the floor.

For all her ursine shape, the Valkyrie did not fight like a bear but rather swayed lightly from foot to foot. Mr. Scant showed no fear, though: after a few moments' contemplation, he went on the offensive. Rushing at the Valkyrie, he aimed his claw at her face.

The giant woman's grin made it clear she lived to fight. She used her cleavers almost lazily to deflect Mr. Scant's attacks: he was striking with one hand, but she could defend with two. When Mr. Scant tried to trip her, she chopped downward—he had to twist away or lose a leg. He was faster than she, but the Valkyrie wasted no movement. Both combatants anticipated the other's strikes, so that the fight really did look like a dance.

Mr. Scant seemed to gain the upper hand with a clever feint, forcing the Valkyrie off-balance, but as he pressed her, she crouched a little—then jumped. Mr. Scant may as well have tried to overpower a locomotive: her metal chest piece knocked back his claw and sent him reeling.

With a ferocious cry, the Valkyrie charged, and for a moment, I lost sight of them both. Then Mr.

Scant came flying through the door into the room that was meant to be my refuge. He skidded across the dusty floor, managing to get back to his feet before he hit the far wall. The Valkyrie flowed in after him, and for the first time, I noticed a sack tied over one of her shoulders, which no doubt contained one very large book. But I could not dwell on that, because with a strange simper, she hacked both cleavers at Mr. Scant's head.

A loud clang rang out as Mr. Scant used the claw to protect himself. A rain of blows followed. "Stay back!" Mr. Scant yelled at me, and all thoughts of trying to help melted away. I was on the wrong side of the crate now, so I darted to a gap between two other boxes.

The Valkyrie formed the solid center of a maelstrom of brutal attacks, fast as a spinning chariot wheel fixed with blades. Mr. Scant kept her at bay, finally managing to escape by launching one blade at the Valkyrie's unarmored leg and forcing her to jump away. She cackled at that, waving one cleaver as though scolding a naughty child, while I was more concerned by the fact the blade had dug into the wooden crate mere inches from my face.

The two fighters hurled themselves at one another

again. Mr. Scant continued glancing at me, which meant he expected something. Then I understood: that spring-loaded claw had not come so close to hitting me by coincidence. Mr. Scant had conveyed it to me. With shaking fingers, I tugged the blade out of the crate. The skin of my hands looked oddly pale, and my face was no doubt as colorless as the clean laundry at a nunnery. Then Mr. Scant lunged forward and grabbed both of the Valkyrie's wrists, holding her still.

"Oho!" she exclaimed. "A test of strength, is it? Want to try to take my throne, ha?"

Mr. Scant tried to stop her, but the Valkyrie began to raise her arms again. She brought her hands together, meaning to lift them above Mr. Scant's head before smashing them down again. I knew I had to act. With a wordless yell, I leapt onto the titan's back, brandishing the detached claw.

With a bellow of surprise that reverberated through my whole person, the Valkyrie dropped down into a squat. This was about the last thing I had expected her to do, and before I knew it, my wrist had been seized by a hand big enough to envelop almost my entire forearm. Panicking, I began to yell, but quickly remembered that Mr. Scant's identity was a secret, resulting in the regrettable exclamation, "*Mr. Sclaw!*"

As I dropped the blade I was clutching, another appeared, pushing into the flesh of the Valkyrie's hand. This blade was still attached to the others on Mr. Scant's claw. He had stabbed the back of the Valkyrie's hand, the first time I had seen him draw blood. The Valkyrie released me with a yell of pain. Using the moment of distraction, Mr. Scant cut open the Valkyrie's bag and snatched the big book from inside. Then he dragged me by the wrist over to the doorway and pushed me into a run—so fast I nearly fell. As we made our escape, the Valkyrie's voice boomed all around us. "Cowards! Two against one! *Stop them!*"

When I tried to wrench free from Mr. Scant, he looked back at me with eyes ablaze. "What are you *doing*?" he demanded.

"We can't run away! We can't let her call us cowards!"

"There's being brave and there's being baited. If you want a chance to prove your bravery, plenty of people are coming to kill us in *this* direction."

He was right. Guards answering the Valkyrie's call had spotted us on the stairs and were charging toward us—men dressed plainly, like gardeners or laborers. I was relieved to see that one of them was the scarred man, until he drew out a small pistol and made a very deliberate effort to shoot Mr. Scant in the face. I had no idea where the bullet went, but Mr. Scant did not stop running and neither did I.

Men fell like a house of cards as we reached them, one tumbling clear off the staircase. Mr. Scant let go of my wrist to knock another man aside, then picked me up once again before sprinting up the stairs. Another shot rang out but did not find its mark. We soon reached the tunnel through which we had originally come, where Mr. Scant dropped one of his canisters that filled the air with smoke. To my surprise, however, we did not fly down the passage to freedom. Instead, Mr. Scant led me slowly toward a place against the wall, inside the smoke.

We heard our pursuers—including the Valkyrie herself—yelling to one another as they ran through the smoke and down the tunnel we had turned away from, chasing our phantoms. When they disappeared, we hurried back the way they had come and toward a different tunnel altogether. I had a comical vision of our pursuers bursting out from underneath Mrs. McBunty and sending her cats flying, but dared not laugh.

The new tunnel was dark, and much longer than the one we had come through. I thought for a moment that I saw light up ahead, four little circles in a row, like the light from a small candle reflecting on spectacles, but they vanished after a moment or two. Then, for a time, there was nothing in this whole world of darkness but me, my father's valet, a metal claw, and an old book of magic.

Finally, we came to a door, and when Mr. Scant opened it, light returned to the world. I let out a sigh of relief and smiled at Mr. Scant in triumph. To my alarm, he met my smile with a look of great and terrible fury.

VII
A Second Mr. Scant

Mr. Scant was very unhappy with me.

I wished I knew why, but our escape took priority over an explanation. The door at the end of the tunnel had opened onto what appeared to be the corridor of a girls' school, and with the school entrance locked tight, we had to leave through a window on the first floor. When I couldn't quite climb onto the windowsill, Mr. Scant defenestrated me. I landed in a bush, which did little to soften my landing, and wondered if Mr. Scant had known it was there or not.

When we were back onto the road and the claw was safely hidden away, Mr. Scant no longer had any reason to hold back his anger. "Please explain to me, Master Oliver, what you were thinking when you *attacked* the Valkyrie."

Of course, it was not Mr. Scant's way to express his anger by yelling and screaming. But his calm, sneering rage distressed me more than any outburst would have. I stopped dead.

"When I . . . ?"

"When you took it upon yourself to attack a woman capable of snapping your neck between finger and thumb? Hmm?"

"I . . . thought you wanted me to distract her. Was that . . . not why you aimed your claw at me?"

Mr. Scant's lips pressed together not once, not twice, but three times before he found the words. "I conveyed one of the blades of my claw to you so that you could approach *stealthily* and cut the book from its sack. It would have been distraction enough to allow for a smooth escape. Jumping up like some rabid hound—you nearly killed us both! Even if had you managed to plunge the blade into her neck, you would very probably now be a murderer. Over something as trivial as an old book. *This* is why we must train your mind first, Master Oliver. This is when sharpness of the mind is paramount. To remove this idea that being brave matters more than being wise. To get away from empty-headed viciousness."

"Well, you don't have to be like that!"

"I will be as I see fit, Master Oliver. I assure you there is much worse I could say—and do."

I didn't like the sound of that, so the rest of our slow march home was underscored by a silence as frosty as the weather. Since Mr. Scant carried the old book, I held the pack with our scarves and the claw inside. Tempted as I was to throw the thing into the stream, I suspected that if I did, I would soon follow it.

"I shall be asking Mr. Ibberts to begin extra observational tasks," was Mr. Scant's parting barb, which I ignored. I made a beeline for my room but found Meg there. She looked up from her dusting and asked me if I was feeling all right.

"I'm just . . . cross that my eyes keep itching!" I snapped.

Meg was tactful enough to nod and say, "I've had itching eyes enough times to know to excuse myself, Master Oliver. Please excuse me."

All of the next day, my foul mood persisted, and Chudley did nothing to help it. He had decided the captain of his big sister's chess team was the most beautiful girl he had ever clapped eyes on, and he kept cooing about how he was going to marry her.

"You were prattling on about this all lunchtime," I said, when he brought it up yet again after school.

"Well! Somebody got out of the wrong side of bed this morning!" said Chudley.

"I'm just tired of hearing about it."

"How could anyone tire of such divinity?" A look of realization crossed his broad face. "Oh!" he said. "Well, well. *Well*, well, well. I see what happened here. I'm sorry you got your heart broken, Ollie, but you must put on a brave face. Stiff upper lip! What's she like? Maybe I can help you get her back."

I blinked at him, but the earnest expression on his silly face made me bite my tongue. "It's nothing like that. Sorry, I have a lot to think about at home."

"Your father's not being a beast to you again, I hope?"

"No! No, he's . . . not really anything to me these days."

"Well, you know you can talk to me if you need to." Chudley's arm landed heavily on my shoulder. "No need to hide in the library with all the dusty books!"

"I like the books," I said, but regarded Chudley thoughtfully. Maybe it wouldn't hurt to be a bit more like him. He always seemed to enjoy life, but it had never occurred to me to *envy* him before. "And you can, er . . . talk to me as well, if you need to."

"Well, in that case I will!" Chudley said triumphantly. "Let's talk about the incomparable pleasure of gazing upon the radiance of Alicia, the Angel of the Chess Team! It takes an artist's eye to see these things, you know. I tell you, Helen of Troy's got nothing on her. And *then* she puts on her glasses, and all I can say is it's a sad thing that those Trojans didn't know the joy of a girl in spectacles . . ."

After Chudley and I went our separate ways, I trudged home, thinking about Mr. Scant until the sound of horses jolted me from my reverie. Coming down the road toward me were two young women in matching hunting habits. Their horses made for fine-looking mounts, and the riders' clothes were ostentatious; gusts of wind pulled at the folds of their skirts bunched up on the side of their respective saddles, which gave the strange impression of the riders traveling underwater. The oddest part—they held fashionable opera glasses up to their faces and peered through them at all they passed, waving hello and then laughing to one another. The riders were far from anywhere that anyone would go hunting, and their odd, unchaperoned excursion left me so bewildered that when they disappeared down the road, I wondered if I had fallen into a dream.

I did not have long to ponder the enigma; a short time afterwards, I heard someone near the pond say in an exaggerated whisper, "Oi, you!"

Peering behind the trunk of a dead tree, I saw that the voice belonged to an old man in a topcoat trimmed with white fur. "C'mere," he said, in a decidedly rough tone. "Really, get y'self over here."

"I . . . think I'd rather go home," I said, and began to hurry away.

"Oi . . . no. You—get back here!"

When I looked back, the man was in pursuit, but the effort needed for a brisk walk appeared to make him puff and blow. He was a thin man and decidedly gaunt: the more I stared at him, the more alarming I found him. A strange shock of white hair sprouted from under his cap, pushing out from underneath the brim like weeds in a poorly kept garden. His bushy mustache was noticeably longer on one side and yellowed by tobacco. All things considered, this was not a man I much wanted to associate with. I readied myself to run.

"Wait!" the man called out, the word half a cough. "Oliver Maximilian Diplexito, son of Sandleforth and Edwina Diplexito, *stop there and listen!*"

That was enough to make me pause. Even if I ran

away, the stranger knew who I was and where to find me. But that didn't mean he wasn't a lunatic.

"Who are you?"

The man stumbled closer, stopping for a few moments with his hands braced against his knees. "Urgh! My name is Reggie. Reggie Scant."

The other Mr. Scant, or more properly *Mr. Gaunt*, had very little in common with his brother. But as he led me to a funny little tearoom so we could have a sit-down and some tea, he told me they were in fact twins. Though both Scant brothers were tall and wiry, I would never even have guessed they were related.

"You're . . . really different from how I expected you to be," I said.

Mr. Scant's brother took a sip of his Earl Grey and then gurgled in horror. "Forgot the sugar," he said. He had been stirring the tea for at least half a minute. "But yes, yes, people would tell us that all the time. Very stiff, was Heck. Whereas me, I liked jokes, pranks. He was the one who enjoyed, oh, you know—lining things up in order of size."

As Mr. Gaunt heaped no fewer than four spoon-fuls into his cup, I tried to remember if I had ever seen another grown-up take sugar in tea.

"Did you say 'Heck'?" I asked.

"Mmm. And now of course he's . . . he's there, doing the gentleman's gentleman bit. Yes? Your father's valet." Mr. Scant's brother scrubbed at the back of his scalp with a hand, which I assumed was a nervous habit. He had taken off his cap when we came into the little tearoom, revealing that his bushy hair didn't start until three-quarters of the way back around his head. "Now, don't you worry now, I'm the only one who knows where Heck works, so I'm the only one who, ah . . . who figured out who the boy was who came with him for the book yesterday. You! It's . . . you. Isn't it, Oliver?"

If he refused to answer my questions, I'd refuse to answer his. "Mr. Scant says you're held against your will. They make you steal—"

"Hushhhh! Shush!" Mr. Gaunt almost sprang from his seat. "There are things to say and things to not say," he whispered, looking furtively at the other patrons in the tearoom, none of whom had paid us the least bit of attention until he had started waving his hands at me.

"Sorry," I said. "It must be hard for you."

His tired eyes blinked at me once or twice, and I wondered how long it had been since anyone had said such a thing to him. Then he gave a little shrug, picking up his teacup. "Things can be difficult. There are ways to manage. But!" He brought his cup down too hard on his saucer, spilling a little tea over the rim. "You're a good boy, Oliver Diplek— . . . *Diplexito*. Yes. I can tell you are. I can tell. You remind me of my Ellie—she's your age. A few years older."

"Your daughter?"

Mr. Gaunt nodded, with a little smile.

"Is she well?"

"She is, I think. I think so." The thought seemed to sober him. He cleared his throat and sat forward, rubbing his hands together. "At the very least, she is *safe*. She's in a university near Paris, where they say she's the most brilliant female mind since . . . since, uh . . . Oh, tip of my tongue." Then he clicked his fingers so loudly it made me lean away. "Since *Maria Agnesi*. They may just be being nice, but that's quite a thing. I'm told. And yes, yes—*yes*! That's why we're here. Because you remind me of her, and we're here to talk about keeping *you* safe. That is important, you know, being safe, and whatever Heck seems to think about . . . about how to protect the young'ins, huh! Doesn't seem to be doing a good job of it, does he, now? Does he? I mean, look at you, stripling of a twig of a lad, and what do I hear? He's taking you down there with the Valkyrie! The Valkyrie, for the love of Mike!"

"I'm not a stripling."

"Oh, no stripling thinks it's a stripling—that's the rules," he replied.

"I wasn't in any danger," I said. "I was only meant to watch, and it was . . . It was my own fault I got in harm's way, because I got it wrong, what Mr. Scant wanted me to do."

"Hearken to you defending him. Look, Heck is my brother even after all that's happened—even now, when he still thinks I need him looking after me. I know him. I've known him a long, long time. Several times as long as you've had in this world, little twig. So you listen to me when I tell you—Heck, he is a dangerous, dangerous man. If you really think he's taking you under his wing for some kind of . . . charitable work, you should think what's in it for *him*. Yes. Heck always has three or four plans going at once, and they *all* bend his way, trust me on that."

I didn't like the sound of that. "What exactly are you accusing him of?"

"No accusations! No accusations. Only thoughts upon which to ponder, butterflies to be chased, so on and whatnot. Beauty is truth, and truth beauty, isn't that it? So both are in the eye of the beholder."

Mr. Gaunt took a triumphant final gulp of his tea. "Consider, when he nurtures your trust, what he stands to gain. What he is lacking. Consider why he chose you and your family. Perhaps think a few years down the line, when young Oliver has some control over the company his father built. Maybe he knows a brilliant but failed engineer, already employed by the family. Maybe he could get that old man a senior position. His fingers in the pies, as it were. Consider that maybe one day he'll be so trusted that if anything were to *happen* to the new head of Diplexito Engineering and Combustibles, *he'd* be the one in charge."

Mr. Gaunt slammed a palm down onto the table for emphasis, rattling the crockery and causing the owner to give him a sharp look. He held up his hands in apology. "Food for thought," he concluded and rose to saunter away. As I was about to call after him, he changed direction and sauntered back before producing a funny little floral purse. "I forgot to pay," he said, drawing out some pennies. And then he turned and left in earnest.

I sat alone, finishing the pot of tea. After all, it wouldn't do to let it go to waste. The tea had yet to cool enough for me to drink without blowing on it, making me wonder if Mr. Gaunt had a tongue made of leather.

He had not been at all as I had expected him to be. More than his eccentric behavior, I thought about his reasons for seeking me out. Did he really come solely to tell me that his brother, Heck—short for Hector, I assumed—was not what he seemed? Perhaps Mr. Gaunt was content with his lot in life and wanted his brother to stop interfering. Could it be true that Mr. Scant had designs on Father's company? I hadn't even considered that I might take over some day. Somehow, I doubted Father would be very keen on that idea. And besides, that plan would move at an incredibly slow pace for someone who could steal whatever he liked.

The conversation also prompted a new worry. If Mr. Gaunt were loyal to his captors, and knew who I was and where I lived, he could quite easily betray not only his brother but me as well. I had to speak with Mr. Scant about this, and so hurried home after I finished the tea.

Without one of his nods toward the Ice House, however, talking with Mr. Scant was impossible. He remained angry with me, and all evening he stayed close to Father. I had to wait until the next day, after I returned home from school. When I determined Mr. Scant was not with Father, I went to the Ice House and cast about for the concealed handle. The door opened, which meant it was unlocked and Mr. Scant was inside. With a new sense of resolve, I ducked in.

A moment later, something very heavy slammed into my chest. Somewhere, a handbell rang, and I heard someone running in my direction. As my vision blurred, I felt a weight pushing down on my shoulder and a knife pressed to my neck.

VIII
Paper Riches

"**I**t's the boy, it's the boy!"

Those words were my salvation. As I heard them, the pressure on my shoulder relented. As I coughed and gasped for breath like a man rescued from drowning, someone began to dust me down: Mr. Scant. Behind him, the scarred coachman took a step back, returning his knife to his belt.

"There, no harm done," said Mr. Scant. "Steady yourself now, boy. Here." He produced something to drink from a hip flask, and I swallowed it without thinking. As I began to cough uncontrollably, Mr. Scant went on: "That should do it. You must excuse Mykolas—he has more to lose being discovered here than even I do."

"Please forgive my caution," the scarred man added, in an accent that might have been Russian.

Mr. Scant cleared his throat. "Since we haven't had one yet, perhaps a proper introduction is in order. Master Oliver, I would like to present Dr. Mykolas Mikolaitis, sometimes known also as the Velinas. He is an expert on the old magicks from the region north of Prussia, currently under occupation. Mykolas, it is my pleasure to introduce Master Oliver Diplexito."

"I hope I gave no offense," Dr. Mikolaitis said with a bow.

"A pleasure to make your acquaintance," I wheezed, offering my hand.

"Forgive me also for the shooting," said Dr. Mikolaitis, squeezing my hand rather too hard. "In the spa, under the ground. I aim to miss, but I must pretend to be a louse to be amongst lice."

"'Lice' is what Mykolas calls the Woodhouselee Society," said Mr. Scant.

"Makes sense, no? Woodhouses, woodlouses, lice."

Once my vision cleared, I saw that I had set off some kind of security apparatus and been knocked to the ground by a large log on a rope. My ribs felt bruised, but at least this mishap had distracted Mr. Scant from his anger over the Valkyrie. "Come, let's get you seated," he said.

Once I we reached the bottom of the chamber and I sat, wincing, Mr. Scant explained that Dr. Mikolaitis was a scholar whose country had fallen to a great empire, a place where the people longed to be free. His father, whose own parents had died in a famous uprising, had wanted nothing more for his own son than for him to escape the empire he'd been born into. He taught the young Dr. Mikolaitis two things—to study and to fight. His father spent his life's savings sending his son to France to study, where young Mykolas's thesis on the pagan gods from the lands around the Baltic Sea brought him to the attention of a member of the Royal Geographical Society. This new benefactor offered Dr. Mikolaitis a position in London. Though Dr. Mikolaitis eagerly accepted, he soon found his benefactor was a member of the Woodhouselee Society. Instead of the life of learning he had hoped for, he was expected to work his way up the ranks of the Society.

"They knew I could fight, so they made me act as their thug," Dr. Mikolaitis told me. "It was a bad time. There is a place in the Yorkshire Dales, the beautiful Yorkshire Dales. You find a river there called the Strid. It looks oh so pretty, but those waters are deep, and they move so quickly that if a man is thrown in, he never comes out again. So easy, to make such things look accidental. I had to tie a man's hands behind his back and walk him there. The professor who had said such beautiful things about my thesis took him from me and pushed him into the river. For the rest of my life, I will see his face when I close my eyes."

"Mykolas decided to write a letter to expose the Society," said Mr. Scant.

"To the *Times*, though in truth, I would never send it," said Dr. Mikolaitis. "They would only call me a lunatic."

"Fortunately, I saw him writing his letter, there at his guard post," said Mr. Scant.

"From above," said Dr. Mikolaitis. "Nobody ever thinks to look upwards."

"This was before the Ruminating Claw, before there was any plan to create forgeries. But I would perform reconnaissance on Reginald's lab, to see him work. There I met Mykolas, and he became my staunchest ally within the organization."

"They tell me very little, and ask very much," Dr. Mikolaitis said, "but I know what to say to please them, and they think my people are weak-willed and obedient, so we are safe."

"Before you let yourself in, we were discussing your mishap with the Valkyrie," Mr. Scant said, and Dr. Mikolaitis laughed such a booming laugh that I felt sure people outside would be able to hear it.

"Yes! You are brave young boy," he said, his smile making his scars twist into strange patterns. "A boy after my own heart, that is how to say it?"

Mr. Scant nodded. "It is. But let us not encourage recklessness. No more launching yourself at dangerous fighters, Master Oliver, unless you want to end up with a face like Mykolas's."

"My face?" Dr. Mikolaitis shook his head at me. "He jokes. My scars, they are from when I am very small, very young child. Well, most of them!" Once again, he laughed as though this were tremendously funny.

"I feel really awful about . . . doing the wrong thing," I said. "I'm sorry. I should have understood. I know what to look out for now."

"Good," said Dr. Mikolaitis. "Sharp eyes will keep you alive. And . . . strong heart!"

"And a strong *mind*," said Mr. Scant. "Mishaps aside, we are making good progress. I only hope there will be no more complications."

"No more complications, that's right," I said—and

hastily began to reconsider mentioning Mr. Scant's brother. Rather to my surprise, I wanted little more than to continue this peculiar apprenticeship, and I would do nothing that could jeopardize it. But even if I chose not to mention the meeting, I couldn't ignore Mr. Gaunt's words altogether. After a bit of thought, I said, "Isn't it a shame you didn't invent something for Father's engines, so you could work in his company?"

"What do you mean by that, Master Oliver?"

"Well, that way you wouldn't have to be his valet any more. You could . . . concentrate more on your brother."

Mr. Scant looked to his friend Dr. Mikolaitis with faint amusement, and Dr. Mikolaitis laughed uproariously. "My dear Master Oliver," Mr. Scant said, "it is not for want of money that I took on this role. Let me show you something."

On one of the nearby platforms sat a large camera, the type with bellows and a sheet the photographer disappears underneath. "Do you know what this is?"

"A camera."

"Note specifically a few discrete points. Here, allowing the particular fit of the lens. Also here, where the aperture can be adjusted. The small parts ensuring a steady hold on the film inside. Each of these elements was somebody's invention. Or perhaps the invention of a group of men. Just as dozens and dozens of parts make up your father's engines, each refined to perfection by a specialist, so too has the work of many men produced these cameras. And in this instance, I was one of these dozens and dozens of men. I am also responsible for certain parts in pocket cameras, in modern gramophones, and in the records they play. Myself, I own a few patents, under various names." Mr. Scant held up a sheaf of papers thick as an almanac.

"Are you telling me . . . you're rich?"

"Rich? Not beside your father, or Mr. Beards, or Mr. Binns. Compared with other valets and butlers? Certainly. But I remain head of your father's household because it is useful."

"It is?"

"It is. This is where I want to be. It is not unusual for me to be in your father's workshops when I need particular tools. I can take parts and materials— with proper payment, of course. And I actually rather enjoy myself. This vocation keeps me active. This may come as a surprise, but Mrs. George has the sharpest ears of anyone I know. Sneaking past her makes for excellent practice. If I could change places with your father, Master Oliver, I would have to decline."

I nodded. Of course, Mr. Scant was capable of convincing lies, but this didn't seem like one of them. Why, then, was his brother so suspicious? Had Mr. Gaunt's captors poisoned his mind? Whatever the case, I needed time to think before I informed Mr. Scant about our meeting.

"Come up here and let's look at the plans of the vaults that Mykolas has brought us," Mr. Scant was saying. I hurried to join them. "Tonight, you must learn the history of the British Museum," Mr. Scant added. "Because, at the soonest possible juncture, I mean to return that wretched grimoire to where it belongs. Which is in a hidden chamber deep underneath the Reading Room."

Dr. Mikolaitis grinned. "Breaking into the British Museum. You get to have all the fun. Try not to die."

IX
Smoke and Flash Powder

By the time we were on our way back to London, I felt almost comfortable with the task ahead. After all, this wasn't the first time I would break into a famous museum.

Diligently, I had done as Mr. Scant asked. I learned that the British Museum was home to the British Library, with most of the books housed in the famous dome of the Reading Room. The museum itself was not only large but continually growing. Mr. Scant said the current construction of a new wing, named the King's Galleries in honor of the late King Edward, would simplify our entry.

Because agents of the Crown kept the library vault hidden from the public eye, Mr. Scant assured me that he did not anticipate any guards. "The grimoires are effectively national secrets. Therefore nothing about their disappearance reached the news-papers," he explained. "The theft happened while the book was under the protection of a member of the Woodhouselee Society, and as such, there is no reason to suspect the Ruminating Claw."

"If it's underground and secret, doesn't that mean getting inside is really hard?" I asked. "If they lock us in, won't we be trapped there forever?"

"Not forever. Another king will need to be crowned some day."

Our carriage was the same growler as before, neatly repaired after our visit to the gallery. Once we reached the center of London, Dr. Mikolaitis stepped down from the driver's seat and thumped me on the chest—his way of showing affection. "Good luck," he said. In the dim light, I could hardly tell his scars from his mouth, but I was fairly sure he had given me an approving smirk.

Unlike the National Portrait Gallery, the British Museum stood in its own grounds, with high iron railings surrounding it. However, some gates had been replaced with wooden ones while construction works took place. Mr. Scant opened them as eas-ily as if they were old broken-down garden fences: after getting us through, he even put the padlock and chain back just as we had found them.

Though I had been to the museum before, I found myself completely disoriented. I would have recognized the main entrance's Ionic columns and stone steps, but this construction site was wholly alien. Mr. Scant seemed to melt into the shadows of the walls, and before I knew it, he had forced open a window. Perched on its sill, he reached down a hand to haul me in from my place on the flagstones.

We dropped into a room that—to my slight disappointment—was filled with coins and pots. Mr. Scant brought out two torches and handed me one before leading the way through the gloom. A few rooms later, as the beams began to fall on enormous dog-headed gods and great blank-eyed, square-bearded faces, I struggled to contain my excitement. The Egyptian collection, *in the dark*. I wondered if this was how the men who explored ancient tombs must have felt, soon to be cursed for taking what was not theirs. Mr. Scant, unsurprisingly, showed no sign of pleasure as he cut through the darkness, scarf up over his mouth and claws cycling like arachnid legs.

Eventually, we came to a window that looked out onto the central court. The Reading Room stood alone there, a round island in the midst of neoclassical cliff-faces. Instead of leading me to it, though, Mr. Scant whispered, "We need to go *up*."

So up we went, taking a wide stone staircase at such a pace that I couldn't help making a lot of noise, though Mr. Scant didn't seem to mind. After a short search, we found a window that pleased him.

"Wait for the rope," he said, then climbed back outside and disappeared further upwards. For a few long moments, I waited alongside a small statue that might have been a lion or a dog, which watched me with rather a judgmental expression. I made an effort to be brave when the rope dropped down, but had the dog-lion been alive, it probably would have chuckled to itself about my hesitation on the window ledge before I stepped off.

As I clung to the rope for dear life, preparing to follow Mr. Scant up to the roof of the building, I made the mistake of looking down to the paving slabs below, where a light mist was playing about the edges of the buildings. I knew that Mr. Scant wanted me to close the window behind me, but I wasn't keen to take a hand off the rope to push it. After one failed attempt, Mr. Scant quite blatantly swung me so that my back did the closing. I wanted to shout at him, but it was too quiet for that. Besides, Mr. Scant then began hauling me up, which made me grateful enough that I made do with a sour expression.

The sourness didn't last long, because when I saw what Mr. Scant had prepared, my face couldn't manage anything other than disbelief. Another length of rope ran from a sturdy-looking flagpole to the roof of the Reading Room. Mr. Scant was testing it to make sure it would take his weight. Though the Reading Room occupied most of the square court, like an ostrich egg in a sparrow's nest, the prospect of crossing from roof to roof still made the gap resemble a yawning abyss.

The way to cross, Mr. Scant explained as he took my torch from me, was to take another short loop of rope, secure it around my wrists, and then use that on the line rather than relying on gripping it by hand. Then I was to swing my ankles up over the line and make my way along like a caterpillar on a twig. It all seemed rather undignified. "Won't your claw just cut the rope?"

"I never cut what I do not mean to cut."

To demonstrate, he sliced down at the rope, and indeed, he may as well have hit it with his bare hand. "The true blade in each claw is actually hidden

within two blunt slats," he explained. "Too dangerous and impractical, otherwise. To bring out the
blades, I must press my thumb to a catch on the side,
like so."

The movement was surprisingly subtle—remi-
niscent of a cat's claws appearing from under soft fur.
Mr. Scant crossed first, and then it was my turn. The
experience went by in something of a blur. Dangling
upside-down meant that I could only see the tumult
of the November sky, rather than the plunge of death
and splattering that awaited me below. Safely across,
I unhooked my feet and Mr. Scant eased me down
onto a ledge. That was when I saw the end of the
rope, attached to one of Mr. Scant's claws, which
was in turn lodged into a wooden window frame. I
turned slightly green, thinking what could have happened had it come loose, but seeing Mr. Scant strain
to work it free reassured me somewhat.

To get rid of the rope we had left behind, Mr.
Scant set it on fire. It must have been soaked in something flammable, because it burned quickly. As I
stood and pondered our escape route, Mr. Scant was
already circumnavigating the dome, peering closely
at the walkway underfoot. After some minutes, he
found what he was looking for: a barely discernable

gap between the wooden boards of the walkway, one that could be pried open with a bit of razor-sharp persuasion. The opening between the boards was small and dark as the flue of a small house, with little ridges all down the edges. From the direction the chute ran, I could see that it followed the outside of the dome, inside the very walls of the Reading Room.

"Climb down slowly and carefully, and make sure your feet have solid purchase at every step," Mr. Scant said, removing his claw and putting it into its little bag. In a complex-looking procedure, he slipped all his long limbs into the tiny space, and then the chute swallowed him up. After a long, doubtful pause, I followed.

It was probably much like what the chimney-sweep boys like the ones in Reverend Kingsley's book used to experience. Darkness and suffocation. Grime coated each handhold; for the first minutes of my descent, I was careful about getting my clothes dirty, but soon I grew too tired. By the time my feet were back on solid ground, I was exhausted. We had descended far enough that we must have been in the foundations of the building, and then we reached a narrow passage leading toward the center of the dome.

The passage widened again, and we emerged into an open space. Mr. Scant turned on his torch again, but I noticed he didn't give me one this time. The torch's beam ate away at a small portion of the darkness, so that we could see that the chamber was round, like the reading room above it; it was also full of books, but the similarities ended there.

There were books in chains and thick sheaves of paper impaled on spikes, as well as several pits surrounded by what appeared to be ash. Unlike the grand, comforting dome above, this space resembled a torture chamber built by someone who really hated reading.

Near the center of this strange and unpleasant place, we found several important-looking volumes on a reading desk. Mr. Scant gave me the torch as he drew the old book from under a strap across his chest. This tome was identical to the one on the desk in front of him, so after a moment's contemplation, he swapped them. Examining the fake grimoire his brother had made, Mr. Scant looked back to me and reached for the torch—then stopped and ducked, just in time to avoid a huge hand wrapping around his neck.

"Argh! I was sure I was quiet enough that time!"

said a familiar voice. A voice that came from a set of lungs I suspected was bigger than my entire body. With a grin, the Valkyrie struck a match on the side of a bookshelf and lit a small lantern. "Let's have a look at you," she said, setting the lamp on the table and carelessly dropping the match. "Ah, brought the boy again, ha? Remember, child, it's dangerous to play with fire, especially with all this old, dry paper around."

The Valkyrie wiped her mouth with the back of a leather-gloved hand. Her cleaver was in her grip, and for a moment, it caught the light from my torch and shone like a clouded moon.

"What do you stand to gain here?" Mr. Scant asked, laying the forged grimoire down at his feet. "We are only leaving the book."

"What do I gain? First, ask yourself what I lost. I lost face when I let you thieve that there book from under my nose. So this is about getting *even*. What I'm after is the blood price."

With that, she hooked her cleaver under an empty reading desk and heaved it toward Mr. Scant. As he pushed me back to safety, he said, "There must be another way in, one she could fit through. Find it. Go!"

With that, he turned to hurl himself back toward the Valkyrie, who laughed at his efforts to force her back. "Silly little matchstick man," she chuckled. "Coming to give me a hug, ha?"

I wanted to stay, partly because I was worried about Mr. Scant, but mostly because I felt I was safer by his side. I still had the torch, so of course I would be easy to find if the Valkyrie won this fight. But I knew better than to disobey. As I nodded, Mr. Scant turned his hand upside-down: when the Valkyrie swung her cleaver, her forearm landed on the point of one claw. Her bellow of pain propelled me along as I scurried away.

The big chamber was as dark as starless midnight, and the torchlight barely cut through it. As I tried to make haste, I made the mistake of looking back toward Mr. Scant and the Valkyrie, and fell into one of the pits. My landing sent a cloud of ash puffing upwards, and I coughed and sputtered as I crawled back out. Lucky that the pit was only a few feet deep. For a moment, my torch flickered, and when I shook it in a panic, the light reflected on something up ahead. I hit the torch until the beam became steady again, then loped forward like a caveman to investigate what I had seen glimmering. When I found it,

I wondered if I had knocked my head in the fall and begun to see things.

A large Egyptian sarcophagus loomed before me, stood upright like an ornate wardrobe. The placid look on the gilded face made me think of a motion picture about King Ramses being brought to life, making me hesitate to step closer. Only when I felt something solid underfoot did I realize the relic stood on a highly incongruous metal platform.

There was nothing else for it: I stepped closer and pulled at the ancient casing. Someone had fitted hinges on the lid, so it opened in the manner of a heavy door, and I breathed a sigh of relief when nothing lurched out to grab me. Instead, a large and obvious lever protruded from amidst the hieroglyphs.

Under the lever was another lamp like the one the Valkyrie had used. The sarcophagus was big enough to accommodate her, so I wondered if this had somehow been the way she had gained access to the chamber. I tried to shine my torch to the ceiling above, but it stretched high enough that the light failed to reach it. I was certain that I stood in the very center of the chamber, though, and between that, the metal platform, and the lever, I reasoned that sarcophagus was a kind of elevator. "That's a bit silly," I mumbled to myself, but with no time to lose, I hurried back to tell Mr. Scant.

When I found him, two of his claws had been snapped clean off, but the Valkyrie wielded only one cleaver. I began to call out, but as I did, the Valkyrie's arm shot out like a piston. She grabbed Mr. Scant by the top of his head. He slashed upwards with his claw, but the cleaver stopped his blades. The Valkyrie began to squeeze, but Mr. Scant stabbed upwards again, this time with the claws of his thumb and little finger. The cleaver deflected the thumb, but the smallest claw found its mark, and the Valkyrie screamed in pain again. Mr. Scant took the opportunity to scramble away.

"Have you found it?" he asked, as though the raging giant behind him did not even exist.

"I think so."

"Good, we should—" Mr. Scant began, but the Valkyrie threw a bookshelf at him. Only a small one, but it nonetheless sent him reeling. "Madam, I would thank you not to interrupt," he said as he picked himself up and dusted himself down.

"I'm going to scoop out your brains and use you as a vase for my geraniums," was the Valkyrie's answer.

Mr. Scant tutted and picked up the Valkyrie's lamp from the desk. As he unscrewed the top and grabbed a handful of scrolls from a nearby shelf, she held up her hand.

"You wouldn't burn someone else's property. Come, now. It's not your way."

"I'm disappointed you don't know me better than that," Mr. Scant said, and let the paper meet the flame. As the Valkyrie lunged forward, he threw the lamp at her, and she screeched as it burst on her breastplate. The oil in the lamp spilt out, and her apron caught fire. As she beat at the flames, Mr. Scant drew out his brother's forgery from where he had strapped it to his chest and dropped it into the flaming oil. "Now, lead the way," he told me.

"Are you *mad*?" the Valkyrie bellowed as we ran. "The place will go up like tinder, ha! Claw! Get back here, Claw!"

Mr. Scant showed no sign of concern. When I led him to the sarcophagus, he grasped its purpose instantly, ushering me in and pushing the lever upwards. With the sound of heavy machinery grinding into action, the platform began to rise. Mr. Scant went to the edge to watch for the Valkyrie, but it was soon apparent that the platform turned as it ascended, as though we stood atop a giant screw.

After reaching a certain height, we began to catch a glimpse of the Valkyrie with each turn. She ranted and raved, telling us to get back down there, which of course we didn't. She had torn away half of her apron and thrown it into one of the pits, along with everything else that had caught fire. A coarse smoke rose from the pit, parts of it green and parts red, whether from dyes or from old magic spells, I could not tell. With the fire contained, the Valkyrie went on yelling and even made little jumps, as though she hoped to fly up after us.

"Lucky she got it all into that pit," I said, waving the smoke away from my face. "It would have been terrible if everything burnt."

"It may surprise you, but of all the enemies I have fought, she is in all probability the most intelligent," said Mr. Scant. "She would never have thrashed about, setting everything ablaze. I suppose trusting her not to do so is my sign of respect."

By now, the smoke was filling the air around us. Even Mr. Scant ducked a little when a sound like a firework popped below us; a colorful stream of sparks flowed from the fire pit. I heard the Valkyrie shouting about idiot magicians and stupid magic tricks.

"Inside the sarcophagus, now," said Mr. Scant. In the ceiling above, I could make out an opening not for the entire platform but only for the sarcophagus itself—and only with its door closed. "Quickly," Mr. Scant added, and we crammed ourselves in. As Mr. Scant shut the door, his bony knees pushed me up against the very edges of the container, but if the Valkyrie fit inside, so could we. The thought of her squeezing in made me laugh.

"Are you crying?" asked Mr. Scant.

"No! I was laughing!"

"What is there to laugh about?"

"I imagined the Valkyrie wedging herself in here."

"Ah."

"I'm not afraid of the dark, you know."

With a jolt, our ascent was complete, and Mr. Scant opened the door. We had arrived in the Reading Room, right in the center. Mr. Scant scanned the space, including the impressive domed ceiling. Finding it silent, he led me to the door, but returned to the sarcophagus and pushed the lever down. "Another mark of respect," he said as the sarcophagus began to descend, a plume of smoke escaping past it through the hole in the ground.

The Reading Room's main door was not locked.

Outside, Mr. Scant dashed across the open space of the courtyard and knelt to peer into the keyhole of the door that led to the museum entrance hall. To reach the main gates, we still had reach the other side of this building. "The key's still in here," he rumbled.

"So you can't pick it?"

"This in fact allows us to proceed with celerity."

"With what?"

"With speed."

Mr. Scant pushed the claw of his little finger into the keyhole, making the key drop to the floor on the other side of the door. He then used that same claw to sweep under the door, pulling the key back with it. In no time, we were through, and Mr. Scant of course took the time to lock the door behind him. To the main entrance we walked, checking all corners before unbarring the big heavy door and letting ourselves out.

We came very close to a clean getaway. Down the stone steps we went, and then Mr. Scant lifted me over the main gates. But the moment Mr. Scant dropped beside me, I heard a youthful voice piping up, "Get it! Get it! Get it!"

I had no time to react. All I knew was that Mr. Scant had grabbed my face and forced me down. A

bright flash lit up the world, and then we were running, running fast away from the museum. Behind
us, the youthful voice chirped, "It was really him! It
was really the Claw! Told you there was smoke, didn't
I? And I was right! We got it! We got the picture!"

X

A Truth Revealed

T his was a different kind of anger for Mr. Scant: one he directed at himself.

The entire drive home to Tunbridge Wells, he brooded, stroking his chin and looking at nothing. If I said anything to him, he pretended not to hear a word—or quite possibly didn't have to pretend. I remembered what his brother had said about plans on top of plans, and I imagined he was thinking of dozens of new ones, depending on what that photograph revealed. Even back at the house, he said nothing but, "Be sure to wash all the ash away before sleeping, Master Oliver."

He remained inscrutable during breakfast the next day, as Father held up the newspaper with our story on its front page. INTREPID PHOTOGRAPHER DUO FOIL BRITISH MUSEUM THEFT, the headline proclaimed—with *Naught Thieved This Time in Latest Ruminating Claw Strike* running underneath. A large photograph accompanied the article—the one that had been taken last night.

While the odd angle and the scarf obscuring Mr. Scant's mouth would make him hard to identify, protecting us from immediate discovery, he cut a peculiar figure. He had lowered his chin into his scarf while looking up into the camera through his bushy eyebrows, making his expression positively demonic.

And then there was me, in the background. Looking for all the world like I had walked straight into the Claw and had been photographed as I toppled over. Although Mr. Scant blocked my face, my collar and one hand were clearly visible. My jacket was indistinct and grubby with soot but nevertheless, there I stood. On the cover of the *Herald*. The bottom of the page even featured a little section in bold about a "mystery child accomplice." The story continued inside the paper, and Father may well have been perusing it as I sat there. I could barely stand it.

"Father, what does it say about the Ruminating Claw's accomplice?" I blurted out. I stole a look at Mr. Scant, whose eyes widened a fraction.

Father folded down the corner of the newspaper and gave me a quizzical look. "You can read it afterwards."

"I wonder what it would be like to do such things," I said. "I expect you would have to be brave."

"Bravery has nothing to do with it, son," Father said, straightening the paper again. "Crime is the coward's way."

I knew not to push him any further than that.

Later in the day, as I went up to my room, Meg told me that Mr. Ibberts was indisposed. That gave me a momentary sense of elation, especially because a cancelled tutoring session increased my chances to speak with Mr. Scant in the Ice House. But Father's valet remained staunchly at his side the entire evening. So I busied myself learning more about Sir Isaac Newton, who—according to Mr. Scant—had secretly written as much on alchemy as on laws of motion and suchlike.

It was not until the next day that I spoke with Mr. Scant again. As I arrived home from school, Meg told me he had asked for a moment of my time in the library. My tutoring session would take place there in any case, so I agreed, but grew curious as I went upstairs to the library door. Inside, I could hear

Mr. Scant and Mr. Ibberts talking together, which struck me as strange. Unable to make out their conversation and deciding there was nothing else for it, I went in.

Upon seeing me, Mr. Scant clasped and unclasped his hands. If I hadn't known better, I would have said he appeared nervous.

"Master Oliver, please sit down."

Glancing between the two men, I took my usual seat.

"There is something we need to discuss," Mr. Scant said. I could not fathom why, whatever he wanted to say, he wanted to say it with Mr. Ibberts beside him. They took seats on the far side of the desk, looking at me as though I were made of glass. As though I might shatter from their very gazes.

"The time has come for the truth," said Mr. Scant. "This can go no further. Regretfully, Master Oliver, everything I have told you these last few weeks, everything about my being the . . . Ruminating Claw—all of it was an invention. A fabrication of ours."

After a few moments' contemplation, I came up with the best answer I could manage: "How do you mean?"

"A few weeks ago, Mr. Ibberts came to me, concerned that you were falling behind in your studies. He said he felt unable to engage you with the world, so . . . we came up with a little ruse. Well, I did."

"No, no," I said. "You can't honestly—"

"The Ruminating Claw is not me and never has been. I have no notion of his identity, truth be told. Your tutor and I had hoped that I could use my past as a performing artist to convince you that . . . that I and the Claw were one and the same. So Mr. Ibberts's son dressed up as an assassin, a friend in the props department of a local theater made me a convincing claw, and we had our play-fight."

Apologetically, Mr. Ibberts produced the dueling sword that the mystery man had wielded that fateful night and placed it on the desk between us.

"The truth is," Mr. Ibberts said in his tremulous voice, "this seemed the best way to inspire you to study."

Mr. Scant nodded. "Never before did you show such interest in your schooling or come so close to fulfilling your true potential."

"But this is ridiculous," I said. "The museums, we . . . How could we . . . ?"

"Ah. The first was a clever bit of stagecraft, you

see. Good friends of mine had already constructed most of the set for a project they had worked upon. It was actually not very accurate. And it was nowhere near the Trafalgar Square you were so keen to see. More recently, I made the mistake of having a fellow I know, a conservationist at the British Museum, help us arrange the jape in the basement. I'm afraid it got a little out of hand when the man with the camera appeared—the wrong place at the wrong time, as they say. Now our picture is on the front of the paper, and things have gone rather too far."

"You're saying that you made the whole thing up?"

"Everything, Master Oliver. And I don't really want to know what the real criminal will make of it when he sees my picture."

"You . . . We . . . could have *died*."

"Yes—we could have. Without a sense of danger, you would never have believed it. But we had much assistance, and we were well-prepared for anything that might have gone wrong. I can honestly say you were in no more genuine danger than you are crossing a road or taking a ferry across the Channel."

"It . . . It makes no sense," I said, shaking my head. For some foolish reason, a lump was forming in my throat. "I met your brother—Reginald. He told me about you when you were young."

"Ah yes. Mr. Bristow is his real name. A very gifted actor. I think he is performing this year in the pantomime at Great Yarmouth."

"Why?" I said. "Why such a lie?"

"To . . . bring some stimulation into your life. We thought it would enrich your time at school, which we both know can be difficult. But . . . well, we should have exercised restraint, Master Oliver. And I am terribly ashamed."

I shook my head. "Stop lying to me."

"That is my intention. I will never lie to you again. I can only beg your forgiveness."

"No! This lie. *This* lie. Stop it. You are Hector Scant, the Ruminating Claw, and I know it."

Mr. Scant smiled ruefully, the first time I had seen him smile at all. "'Hector' is not my name. I know this is a terrible thing to learn. But take solace in what a model student you have become."

"For a *lie!*" I yelled. And with that, something in me changed. I realized I had to believe one of two things. Either I had been apprentice to a master criminal, or I had been deceived by my father's valet. Put like this, the confession no longer seemed so absurd. "All that for the sake of *school*?"

"For the sake of your future," said Mr. Scant.

I banged both fists on Mr. Ibberts's desk, rattling the pens in his pots. When that didn't change the world, I stormed out of the room.

Mr. Scant's admission had stunned me into white-hot anger. I went to my room and tore up the book on Mr. Newton. Finding no satisfaction from that, I attacked my pillow with my fists and teeth and fingernails until I was exhausted. I lay on my bed, panting, thinking those same thoughts I used to have when I threw tantrums at five years old: would they be sorry if I suffocated myself? Would they understand me if I went downstairs covered in cuts and bruises? Should I run away and never come back?

Then came the less absurd questions. What if I went to the papers to identify the man in the photograph? What would the real Claw do if that happened? Should I tell Father what Mr. Scant had done, what he had made *me* do? Would Father give him the sack? Or, more likely, would Father call me a fool and laugh?

As I often did when upset, I sought solace with Mother. I found her in the lounge and hurried over to her, laying my head on her lap and ignoring all her soothing questions. I knew she didn't mind my silence. "Could it be the girl he was courting didn't return his affections?" Mother cooed to her old maid, Mrs. Winton, who knew she wasn't expected to answer. "He grows up so fast, I hardly know what to do with him," she went on, stroking my hair. And there, in that safest and most familiar of places, I let myself drift into a troubled sleep.

I woke up hours later on the chaise longue. Mother was gone, but she must have laid me down gently enough not to wake me. I didn't know the time, but nobody had put me to bed, so it could not have been very late. Darkness had set in, but in November the sun went down early.

Seized by a new determination, I stormed down the main staircase and to the front door, where Penny spotted me. She called out my name, but this only inspired me to start running. I darted down the steps to the drive, and then onto the road and on, and still on.

All the way to the town center I ran, not caring where I was going. If I ran far and hard enough, I thought, I might be able to escape from myself. Was I being a spoilt crybaby? No matter. I would return home before my absence troubled Mother, and most likely Penny would give me an hour or two before saying anything. Perhaps she would mention my leaving to Mr. Scant, but what would he do? He was just an ordinary man.

The clocks had not yet struck nine, so life and activity still filled the town, though a distressed-looking schoolboy with no chaperone drew a few concerned looks. I made my way to the High Street and pressed on until almost the end of the road, and then stopped, out of breath. Looking up, I saw I stood under a spectacular arrangement of glass and light high up above me. It was the fashionable Nevill Café, up above Godkin's Chemists, its glass facade outshining the moon.

As I peered up at the people laughing and drinking there, a young man only a few years older than me came jogging up with a deferential expression. He was dressed like a waiter, so no doubt worked in one of the nearby restaurants, though his trousers ran a little too short and I could see his socks. He tugged on my sleeve to get my attention: "Sir, the gentlemen are asking for you."

"I beg your pardon?" I said.

"Mr. Binns—he asked that I fetch you."

Mr. Binns, Father's business associate, was joint owner of Beards and Binns Financial Services and

Dirigibles Ltd. It would have been rude to refuse him after he sent the waiter to fetch me, so in something of a daze I nodded, and the young man led me into the very café I had been gazing up at. Various men milled about the place, rather than sitting and dining as I would have expected. The proprietors had provided an area close to the windows for the gentlemen to smoke, and I met Mr. Binns in the thick of the haze. He was contributing to the cloud with a thin cigar, and gestured at me with a stout brandy glass. "It *is* you. Sandleforth's boy! I knew it."

"Yes," I said. "Hello, Mr. Binns, sir."

"Now, none of that," Mr. Binns said, putting his fingers around the back of my neck in what he must have thought was an affectionate manner. "No need to call me sir. I'm not your teacher. Call me Roland."

I could think of few things that would make me more uncomfortable that didn't involve spiders, so I said nothing.

"Now, I know Sandleforth and Edwina have raised you well. They keep a good eye on you."

"I hope so, sir," I said.

Mr. Binns rolled his eyes, but the smile returned in an instant. "How about 'Rolly,' if that's easier? Hmm? Think of me as one of your chums. Your father is always talking about you, his worries about how you're turning out."

"He does? I mean, he is?"

"Oh, yes. So tell me—what is the young Diplexito scallywag doing out on the High Street in a daze when good children are home getting tucked into bed, hmm? Should I be concerned?"

"No, Si— . . . No, Mr. Rolly."

"I have a son a few years older than you," he said, accidentally breathing smoke in my face as he turned to face me. "His name is Aurelian—that was his mother's idea. He's away at boarding school, but we get on very well. And the reason for that? I ask him to think of me more as a chum than his father. And I'd like you to think of me as a chum too."

"Er . . ."

"Strange as it may seem to you, Oliver, I was your age once, not so long ago. And I remember wanting so much to become a man. To leave behind boyhood and run wild in the night! Wild with ambition! Oh yes. So I can tell there's something on your mind. Perhaps I can help."

Mr. Binns smiled, a smile that looked as though it had been practiced in the mirror: it was polished to a gleam, but it didn't reach his eyes.

This is a clever businessman, I reminded myself. *He's probably ten or fifteen years younger than Father—so he will still be around after Father retires.* But that smile said he knew that even if Father passed away, his son might still be around.

None of this would have occurred to me only a few weeks ago. Bitterly, I reflected that Mr. Scant's efforts had only made me a cynic. "It's nothing, really," I said. "I'm just having a difficult time at school."

"Oh, I had a hard time in school too," said Mr. Binns, shaking his head. "But look at me now! School is for mathematics and Latin and not looking like a complete fool—the rest is *nous*." To emphasize this, he tapped his forehead.

"Sometimes I worry I don't live up to Father's expectations," I confided. "I'm afraid he thinks I'm . . . not brave enough. I don't want to disappoint him."

"Ah, well, I wouldn't trouble myself too much if I were you. That's just Sandleforth. Sandleforth . . . he's from the old days, you know? The glory days, where men were taught never to look at themselves, never to feel guilty about a thing. And don't I envy that? But who amongst us, who among the *living*, could match the expectations of a man like that? Don't you trouble yourself, my dear boy."

"The problem's that I'm not as clever as him," I said. "I never know when people are lying. Father never has that problem."

"Hmmm—no, you're right, there. He's got a knack for that. Something I wouldn't mind having myself. Here, this will help. Have a nip of this."

"I don't like brandy, thank you."

"Ah! He already knows his tastes. A man of the world. But have you tried *this* brandy?"

Our conversation had started to remind me of a visit from one of my great uncles. They found it hilarious to give me aperitifs and watch me cough and splutter too. If having a sip was the only way to make Mr. Binns drop this idea, I would have to go through with it. Reluctantly, I took the glass.

"Ahoy, look there!" Mr. Binns exclaimed. He spun me around a quarter-turn and stepped in beside me. A flash blinded me, in a sudden recreation of what had happened with Mr. Scant. Only this time, my face wasn't hidden at all. Somebody had taken a photograph of us—a camera sat atop a tripod, and the chap behind looked very pleased with himself. I frowned at Mr. Binns.

"Why would you want a photograph?" It would be a picture of the two of us, Mr. Binns with a cigar and me with brandy, no doubt posed like the best of friends.

"Oh, it's a little service they have here. Don't you worry—they go around to everyone. All good fun."

I found it hard to believe him. Did he want to blackmail me, threatening to show this photograph to Father? Or would he use it later, to show some boardroom what great friends we had been since I was young? "I think I need to get home," I said, pushing his brandy back into his hands. "It's late, and I'm not meant to be here."

"Perhaps you're right. Shall I walk back with you?"

"No, thank you. I'm quite capable."

He chuckled. "If you say so. If you ever want to come back, I'm here every Wednesday and Friday! Hiding from the wife, don't you know? Next time, we can do the rounds with some introductions."

I smiled and gave a half-nod, half-bow that I hoped committed me to nothing. Then I slipped away, watched closely by the young waiter. Hurrying back home, I soon began to feel incredibly tired. Everyone thought me to be a gullible child, to be lied to and made into a laughingstock. I wanted to fall asleep and wake up before any of the debacle with Mr. Scant had happened. But that was no more possible than rubbing away the stench of tobacco that had followed me home like a hungry puppy. I already envisioned Meg collecting my clothes while I bathed and smelling the smoke on them. A few days later, Mother would take me aside and have a talk about the dangers of making friends with the wrong sorts of boys.

When I was in the bath, the frustrations of the day slowly melted away and I began to feel better. Perhaps, I thought as I dipped my head under the water, I would tell Mother that Mr. Scant had given me tobacco and that he ought to be fired. But I didn't suppose she would believe that—it simply wasn't what a gentleman would do. After the bath, wrapped in towels, I stared at myself in the mirror. And the boy who stared back at me looked so infuriatingly ordinary, dull, boring, mundane, and uninteresting that he disgusted me. I picked up the brass soap dish, and—inviting the interesting life that seven years of bad luck could bring—threw it as hard as I could at my reflected self. The shards fell crashing and tinkling onto the tiled floor. I waited until every last one had fallen before replacing the soap dish, stepping out of the bathroom door, and yelling for Mr. Scant.

XI
A Gray World

T he broken mirror changed nothing. Mr. Scant called for the twins, and they dutifully cleaned up the mess. Mr. Scant remained aloof the whole time, and the vague story about slipping and hitting the mirror with my elbow raised no suspicions with Mother and Father. This only irritated me further; I had hoped, at least in part, that they would question me until the truth came out. But they didn't, and it didn't, and I was left with only a resentful numbness.

After my brief visit into a false but spectacularly colorful world, I had lapsed back to my unremarkable life. Everything returned to gray, devoid of warmth or excitement.

To make my mood worse, I continued to see Mr. Scant every day in his role as Father's valet and the household butler. At mealtimes, I daydreamed of being able to expose and embarrass the Counterfeit Claw. I even began to drop hints to Father that the coal bunker concealed a large underground space he knew nothing about. However, in order to understand my hints, Father would first have to consider that I could know something he did not.

School, meanwhile, vexed me more than ever. Everyone had noticed I was doing better in tests and was less likely to be embarrassed by unexpected questions from teachers. Skipper Percival, my Head of House, actually confided in me that I might be prefect material now that I had pulled my socks up. "Thank you, but I'm not sure I really see that in myself," I said. Skipper probably thought I was being modest.

In fact, I was desperate to disprove that Mr. Scant's deception had resulted in any improvement whatsoever—so much so that every word of praise felt like a slap in the face. Mr. Endmarsh's delight that I knew about Pythagoras before he even began his lesson—a slap. The librarian asking why I hadn't been coming lately, because she had been so happy to see someone eager to learn—a slap. Chudley saying everyone called me a swot now—a slap, accompanied by a literal one as well. But while I didn't want to validate Mr. Scant's plan by being a better student, pretending I didn't know the answers made me feel no better.

As for Mr. Ibberts, his tutoring sessions were the same as ever, only now, rather than thinking him a halfwit, I thought him a manipulative schemer. As he blathered on, I wondered if he had dreamt up plots for other children he had tutored. I doubted it, because who would be as credulous a fool as me?

For my first two tutoring sessions after Mr. Ibberts admitted what had happened, I managed to keep up a look of great hatred throughout. But after that, I lost the will and resorted to simply sitting like a dead thing, as if a vampire had sucked all the life out of me. Which was more or less how I had previously sat in Mr. Ibberts's classes, the only difference being that now I usually knew everything he was trying to teach me in advance. We never spoke about the Ruminating Claw again, but then, despite the endless torrent of words running from his gray lungs to my ever-grayer brain, we had never truly *spoken* about anything.

The photograph of the Claw had intensified public interest in the villain. For a while, Scotland Yard promised an investigation into the identity of the young accomplice, but with no solid information to work with, the detectives soon fell silent on the matter. Police artists produced sketches of what the Claw ought to look like without the camera's distortion, and though they thankfully looked nothing at all like Mr. Scant, almost all showed an older man. I wondered if the real Claw took offense at these sketches of someone else altogether. After a week of these reports, I began to fret about whether or not we had hindered the investigation into a real thief.

One paper interviewed the father and daughter who had taken the photograph, who were very pleased with themselves—in their version of the story, they had bravely put themselves in danger to try and keep the Claw from escaping. The fee they earned from selling their photograph had allowed the father to replace his old-fashioned flash-lamp with an expensive new one that lit its powder with electric sparks, and he was quoted as being "happy as Larry." The interview ended with a lengthy description of how to find their portrait studio, which made me wonder if they wanted a visit in the night from the real Claw.

Several times, I found myself wandering to the

Ice House, perhaps to find some evidence that I'd then slip to Father. However, the door—such as it was—had been locked tight. On my fourth or fifth visit, on a day so cold that sleet was falling throughout the garden, I went so far as to try forcing the door open, but it would not budge. Instead, my labors had an effect similar to the rubbing of a magic lamp.

"I should exercise caution if I were you, Master Oliver," said the djinn I had summoned. "You remember Mykolas's little traps, do you not?"

I narrowed my eyes at Mr. Scant, now a well-practiced expression on my part. Any contrition he had previously shown was long gone.

"Father ought to know what's going on in his garden," I said.

"Should he manage to open the door, I assure you that I'll adopt the appropriate look of surprise. Quite as though I had nothing to do with it."

"How much of it was lies? About your brother? About how you both loved science?"

"I have a brother. As children, we were very much interested in becoming men of science. The kernels of truth in the story were there—but alas, they did not grow in such fantastical directions."

"Are you happy you made me look such a fool?"

Mr. Scant said nothing for a moment, then stepped closer and laid a gloved hand on my shoulder. "I set out to make you a better student, and we succeeded beyond our expectations. In that respect, I am pleased. But for a time, I really thought I might be able to consider you a friend. My first in many years. And my youngest. I sincerely regret that I destroyed that possibility."

"If you want to make friends with someone, don't start with lies," I said.

Mr. Scant nodded. "This is why your poor exam results were so worrisome to your parents," he said. "You so often remind us that you are wise beyond your years."

Content with that, Mr. Scant turned toward the house, leaving a trail of light footprints through the thin layer of snow. I stayed where I was for a few minutes more, wishing the snow would settle upon me but watching it melt away. Then I gave the hidden door a smart kick and went to sit on top of the coal bunker.

For a time, the world was silent. I sat alone like Mr. Wilde's selfish giant, in a winter of my own creation. After some ten or twenty minutes of feeling sorry for myself, I heard the sound of horses' hooves.

A few minutes later, the riders came into view—the two peculiar women I had seen before. Once again, they were playing their game, peering all around them with opera glasses held up to their eyes. On horseback, they could see over our garden wall, and from my perspective, they looked oddly like puppets operated from below.

To my surprise, the smaller of the two women turned her opera glasses to me. Her face lit up with pleasure, and she waved enthusiastically. When I only raised a hand in response, she pouted and then blew a kiss. The taller woman raised a fan and gave her companion a reproachful slap on the shoulder with it, and the two of them laughed together. Through all of this, neither lowered her glasses even for an instant.

Once the riders were gone, I flopped back onto the snow, ignoring the cold on the back of my head. My life's path stretched out clearly before me—good results in exams; a job with numbers and sums, day after day; a family of my own to quietly grow old with. No more adventures in hidden libraries or fights with mad, cleaver-wielding women. The library had been a stage, anyway, and the Valkyrie merely one of its players. I would join the ranks of

Ibbertses, spending my evenings in contemplation of interest rates. The world was gray, and all of its lines were straight and clean and rigid and unbreakable.

Which is why I somewhat welcomed being grabbed on the way home from school the next day by a wild-haired and wide-eyed man in a raincoat.

XII

The Sound of an Axe on Wood

T he false Mr. Reginald Gaunt raved and gabbled, shaking me by my shoulders.

"I found you! Thank the Good Lord. Thank the Good Lord God! Boy, boy, listen to me, boy! You *have* to."

"Mr. Bristow, wasn't it?" I said.

"I . . . no. What? No. I'm Reggie Gaunt. Born Reginald Scant. Why would . . . *what*?" He let go of me to take off his cap and scrub at his shock of hair. "How can you forget that? Reginald. Gaunt. Me."

I shook my head. "I don't know if they haven't let you know, but you don't have to keep up the act. Mr. Scant told me."

"Act? Act? Wh-wh-wh—? He told you what?"

"He . . ." I hesitated. "He said you were an actor . . . and you were only pretending. That he wasn't the Claw at all, and that it had all been a trick."

"Oh, you little fool! And you believed *that*? No trick. This . . . *trick* was the trick! He's lying. About having lied to you before! Oh, that is very like Heck. That bounder. *Bounder!* No. *Listen.* You have to listen. Why are you laughing?"

"I hardly know myself," I said, but I couldn't stop. Delight bubbled up like badly poured soda water. Reggie Scant's wild eyes and his obvious, undeniably bizarre character. The realization that my world was not gray after all; Mr. Scant had only painted it that way. And I had fallen for it.

"Get a hold of yourself, boy! Are you mad?"

"Ha! *You* saying that to *me*!"

"Stop this at once!" Mr. Gaunt demanded. "This is why I'm happy we never had a boy. Will you shut up a moment and listen? *Listen!* Oliver! They have captured my brother and he is in *grave danger*."

That stopped my laughing. "What?" I said.

"They have taken him! The men who employ me. And you know what sort they are! They worked out who he was and they *took* him."

"How? I mean . . . where?"

"That Valkyrie woman, no doubt. I don't know the particulars. What is important is that he has been caught and is in some very hot water. Possibly in the literal sense."

"What can we do?"

Mr. Scant's twin had turned deadly serious: he spoke with such intensity I feared he meant to mesmerize me. "This is very important. Heck must have a base of sorts. A lair, a den—somewhere he keeps his claw."

"Yes!"

"You know it! Excellent. We must go at once and fetch that claw of his. The Valkyrie could never have bested him if had it. We must convey it to Heck if he's to have a fighting chance."

"Right! Okay! I'll grab it."

"Let's go."

Reginald Gaunt was not as fast as his brother, and he puffed hard as we ran back toward the house, but I didn't let him rest—not when Mr. Scant depended on us. True, Mr. Scant had lied to me—he even had Mr. Ibberts play along—but I saw now that the close call with the photographer had made him fear for my life if I were identified.

But now he needed me.

We arrived, breathless, at the house, and even though Mr. Scant's brother stopped to catch his breath at the gate, I went back to pull him on by the sleeve. Through the garden we went, until we arrived at the Ice House.

"This is it," I panted.

"This? This . . . what?" managed Mr. Gaunt.

"If you look here, there's a ring. Mr. Scant has a key."

"Can we get inside without it?"

"Well . . . I don't know," I said. "We'd have to force it."

"The two of us? Oh, you must be joking. Ha! It's not as easy as all that, you know. But don't you worry, one of the lads will be bringing a big old axe. Better hope it doesn't get any attention from the house. Shouldn't think it will. It's good and hidden from view. Ahhh. That was too much running."

"Wait—lads?"

Mr. Scant's brother straightened up and stretched his back out. "Yes, my boy. The lads. I imagine they're—ah yes, here they come now."

If I swallowed the anchor from the biggest ship in His Majesty's fleet, I could hardly have had more of a sinking feeling in my belly.

There were a dozen of them or more. Perhaps fifteen men in all, crossing the lawn with looks of murderous intent. Each had a weapon in hand, from cricket bats to hunting rifles. As Mr. Gaunt had predicted, two of them bore wood-chopping axes.

"What is this?" I said, though really I knew and hoped desperately that asking the question would somehow stop it from coming to pass. The other Mr. Scant ran a hand down his sorrowful face and slapped his own cheek.

"I'm sorry to do this to you, boy. But you know I don't have a choice, don't you? You're probably best off running inside your Father's house, really. That's what I'd do if I were you."

"What have you *done*?"

"Well, don't ask me how, but they rather got wind of you. Probably the Valkyrie noticed something. They somehow cottoned that I knew a thing or two I wasn't telling them, and really, that was that. I don't get much of a chance to keep secrets, you see. I'm terribly sorry, my dear boy, but, mmm . . . now that you've led us here, there's really not much other choice. No stopping it now, I'm afraid."

"So nothing's happened to your brother?"

Mr. Gaunt's eyes widened. "Keep it down. They still don't know we're related. And be careful not to call me 'Scant.' To these men my name is *Gaunt*. As for Heck, well, I haven't the foggiest where he is."

By then, the Society thugs were within earshot. With a nervous smile, Reginald indicated the door of the Ice House. "Yes, over here, lads. There—that's the one. Careful, though. Probably booby trapped. Approach like the lair of a wild beast! Sorry. I'll shut up now. Yes. Pardon me. Woo! That was a bit violent. Careful how you swing that. Now, Oliver, you come here now. Come stand out of the way, there's a good lad. Before they hurt you."

"Let go of me!" I yelled, pulling away and running toward the man swinging his axe at the door. Someone else grabbed me from behind before I reached him, and a second later, I found myself lying on the wet grass a few feet away, my head ringing.

"You can't stop them," Mr. Gaunt said, helping me up. "Might as well try to block the Nile with your hands. It really is in your best interest to get away from here. This lot might just decide to ignore their orders to leave you unharmed. Make you an addition to their next dogfight. Nasty business. Not that I'm suggesting we do that! Not suggesting that, okay, lads? Heheh. No. But they've tossed lads younger than you in there. So *watch it*."

"Stop them," I whispered, low enough that only he could hear me. "*Please* make them stop."

He looked into my eyes for a moment and then gave a small, helpless shake of his head.

With a final grunt of effort, the two men with axes forced their way through the door and kicked the remains into tinder. The moment the door fell away, it set off the tree stump on a rope, which smashed into one man and sent him sprawling. The others just laughed at him, then cut down the stump and pushed inside. The brute who had been knocked down soon recovered and followed the rest, leaving me alone with Mr. Scant's brother. Mr. Gaunt appeared to care nothing at all for my repeated pleas.

"*Stop* asking the impossible, you idiot child. Don't you think this is tearing my very soul to shreds? Do you think this is what I *want*? This is what I'm forced into, if I don't want my family to suffer. Now for once in your life, listen. *Listen*. Go back in the house. Do not argue. Do not try to make a difference here, because you cannot. If Heck comes home, make sure he does not cross paths with these men. And then *stay hidden*. Because if one of those troglodytes realizes that they can use you to get to Heck, that's the end for you. Keep causing problems, and my story that you're some errand boy Heck is manipulating won't last. So go. Go now. *Go!*"

He gave me a push, and once I began running, I don't think I could have stopped if I tried. I ran until I collapsed in my room, in my own little protected world. I could not see the men from my window—the Ice House wasn't visible from any window of the house, as I'm sure Mr. Scant was aware—but I could see the gate, so I could watch for when the men left. They departed after almost an hour, laughing and congratulating one another. Mr. Gaunt followed them meekly, lingering a moment at the gate and removing his hat as though someone had died. When I glimpsed smoke above the trees that hid the Ice House from me, the reason was obvious. The men had put all Mr. Scant's belongings to the flame.

XIII
Razed

After I was sure the men were gone, I somnambulated down to the Ice House to watch the smoke. The fire burned less fiercely than I had expected, and when only a little rivulet of smoke still rose from the doorway, I stepped inside to see what remained. As I had feared, the men had destroyed everything but the staircases they needed to reach the next thing to smash. The papers and furniture had been thrown into a pile and burnt; the charred remains still smoldered in the center of the chamber. The top of the dome was stained black, a hellish inversion of a snow-capped mountain.

Mr. Scant found me hugging my knees and watching his papers crumble into ash. I didn't acknowledge him as he descended, pretending I was insensible. That would have been easier. His touch on my shoulder fell gently, more gently than I thought he was capable of, and I looked up.

"Men from the Society came and burnt everything," I said.

"They did."

"I couldn't stop them."

"You are safe, and that matters far more, Master Oliver."

"They even burnt your rocking chair. You loved that chair. You never said so, but I knew you did."

"I did. It belonged to my mother."

I buried my head in my arms again. "This is all my fault."

"No . . ."

"It *was*! Don't you dare pretend you don't think it was! All of it. I led them here. I thought . . . I was so happy when your brother told me it wasn't all lies. But I was foolish, I-I . . . didn't think, I led him straight here when he said you were—"

"Hush . . . hush now, I know. Mykolas told me what happened. Come on, let's get you up."

I didn't resist as he helped me to my feet, but seeing him try to disguise the anguish on his face, I felt a lance of shame pierce through my chest. "I'm so sorry," I said, through a tight throat.

"Master Oliver, I mean it when I say you have nothing to be sorry for."

"But I do." Not thinking about what I was doing, I stepped forward and touched my forehead to the front of his shirt. "I could have stopped them. I'm so, so sorry . . . I couldn't do a thing because I'm completely and utterly useless."

"There was no way you could have stopped them," said Mr. Scant. "I am grateful you did not try. You have come through this unscathed, so the situation is far from the worst it could have been."

"They destroyed everything!" I shouted. "Your machines, your drawings . . ."

For the first time I could remember, Mr. Scant laughed. In all likelihood, it was a false laugh, meant to cheer me, but the sound alarmed me more than anything else—rattly and charnel enough to evoke a skeleton coming to life. I drew back from him with a frown.

"The 'drawings' were not important," he said. "None of them were new, and all the schematics that were worth anything had been sold long ago. You need not concern yourself with those. Machines can be remade. These objects may seem meaningful when we attach memories to them, but when the objects have gone, the memories yet remain."

"They even took your claw."

"Ah yes." Mr. Scant walked away to where his claw had always stood on a table, now destroyed. "That is a shame, but the Claw was not me—and I was not the Claw. Which I mean in a different sense from what I said before. I am sorry for deceiving you. After the photograph, well . . . I realized how careless I had been, to risk putting you in danger. And now I fear it may be too late."

"It is too late," I said. "It's been too late to keep me out of danger for a long time, Mr. Scant."

"There were other ways," said Mr. Scant. "Other means of addressing Reginald's situation. Well, no matter. You are right—it is too late. And for that reason, we must use this opportunity. The Claw is gone, and that must mark the end to it."

"What do you mean?"

"Reginald will have to look after himself now. According to Mykolas, that's what he wants anyway. Oh, I know all about his part in this. My own brother didn't even stop them burning Mother's chair. The Society has sent a clear warning, and it is in my interest to heed it."

"Who are you?"

"Master Oliver?"

I went up to him and gave him a shove, making him stagger back a little. "Who are you? You're not the Mr. Scant I know."

"I understand your anger . . ."

"No, you don't! Where's *your* anger? Look what they've done!"

"I know perfectly well what th—"

"Your brother *needs* you. Now more than ever. *I* need you. And you talk about running away?"

"It's the best chance we have of keeping you safe."

"No, Mr. Scant. The best chance we have is for you to stop feeling sorry for yourself and remember you're the bloody Claw! They're more afraid of you than you are of them, don't you understand that? You're *strong*. And . . . and all my life, I've had people telling me I'm weak. Or worse, *not* telling me, but making sure I know that's what they think. I'm small, I'm cowardly, I'll never be my father. And you're the only one who ever let me even *try* to be anything else. And now you want to run away? This is the time to strike, while they think you're broken. Set your brother free. Who cares what they try to do to you? If they threaten to hurt your niece, you go to France and you take her back too! You can do it. And you know why I'm sure of it? Because you have me to help you. So stop moping around and start getting yourself ready!"

After a long silence, Mr. Scant shrugged.

"When you put it like that . . ."

<hr />

A new plan of action was born—and grew up fast. Mr. Scant stalked about his wrecked lair, scavenging what he could—a steel cord here, a dented piece of metal there—while expounding upon the task ahead.

"As you know, Reggie is not held in bondage but can come and go as he pleases. What complicates the matter is that he has lived with his wife for many years in what she thinks is a comfortable house provided by a university. They are in fact in an open prison. Their daughter, Elspeth, is the trump card the Society can play to keep Reggie in line. If she is in danger, we can move to protect her, but only when it becomes necessary. On the other hand, we must be sure to free Reggie's wife, Winifred, at the same moment as we free Reggie, or the Society will use her to undermine our efforts. Reggie will surrender at the least danger to her person, so securing her is imperative. Of course, removing Winifred from what she sees as her home will be no easy task. So do you know what we shall do?"

"What?"

"Make her disappear upwards."

"Is that really the best way?"

"I promise you that it is."

"Is this going to be dangerous?"

"Oh, our chances of dying will be drastically greater than before," Mr. Scant said, returning to his scavenging. "But the chance of exposure to photographers, even those with the Devil's luck? Minimal."

"So, erm . . . you're more worried about photographers than death?"

"If you want to be safe, Master Oliver, please remain at home. If you leave the house with me, it is entirely possible you will not come back. Not even in your coffin."

"I'm not afraid of dying."

"You ought to be. It would be a terrible waste, throwing away your future just because you think it would impress your father. There—this will work."

Mr. Scant held several of the sharp pieces of metal he had scavenged against his right hand, fixing them in place with wires. The result did not resemble the claw he had lost—it looked rather more like a circle of silver icicles—but he seemed pleased. "We may not stop childish rich men from their games of theft and magic, but we can at the very least stop the one who uses my brother as a pawn."

"So we don't just go to rescue your brother, we go after the ones who ruined him?"

"Indeed. And perhaps we can use a little magic too. Like so." Mr. Scant covered the makeshift claw with his handkerchief. Then, after a moment, he said, "Behold!" and pulled it away again.

It took me a moment to realize what I was looking at. When I did, I went, "Ah!" Mr. Scant had his original claw, as good as new, perhaps even more polished than usual. "You can't have just made that from scraps!"

Mr. Scant smiled and held up the makeshift claw, still half-covered by his handkerchief. "Of course not."

"But they destroyed it!"

"A little good fortune amidst all this destruction," said Mr. Scant, cycling the blades hypnotically. "With the machines at the Ice House, I can sharpen and tune my little friend—or rather, I *could*, prior to today—but mending the damage from my last run-in with the Valkyrie required more specialized equipment. Extraordinarily good fortune that during the destruction, I was working on my claw elsewhere."

"If you have your real claw, why are you cobbling together a new one?"

"All in good time."

"It's not for me, is it?" I asked. "I don't want to be the Junior Claw."

"If I wanted you armed, Master Oliver, it would be with a pistol or a knife. I very much doubt you would have the first idea what to do with my claw."

"And far less with a pile of rubbish you've got strung together."

"Then it pleases me to tell you that you shall have nothing to do with it. Now go and fetch your coat and scarf. We're off to see a man about a balloon."

❦

The man in question was, as it turned out, Mr. Flint, the valet of Mr. Beards—of Beards and Binns Financial Services and Dirigibles Ltd. Though we were told Mr. Flint's duties left him indisposed to see us, Mr. Scant left a message at the trade door, which passed from the cook to the butler to Gerty

Beards's governess and thence to Mr. Flint himself, who quickly excused himself and came downstairs. Mr. Flint appeared to have a great affection for Mr. Scant, and even embraced him, chuckling as people do when they see a dear friend after a long separation. The two of them shared a short exchange in hushed tones, and then Mr. Flint hurried off, coming back with a large iron key. He handed it over to Mr. Scant and patted him on the shoulder—and like that, our business was done.

"How do you come to be such chums with that Mr. Flint?" I asked.

"He came into his position at my recommendation," said Mr. Scant. "The fellow most like me that could be found—that was the unspoken request. And he was just that—once we hushed up his past as a convicted safecracker, of course. Not that Mr. Beards would be overly troubled to learn that particular facet of the man's past. Flint served his time and repented more sincerely than any man I've ever met. A very good mind in that head of his, and an eagerness to do his job to perfection."

Though I felt prepared for our operation to begin then and there, Mr. Scant led me home again and told me to sleep well, for he would be waking me before dawn. He had much more to arrange, and when I asked if he wanted help, he said, "I simply wanted them to see your face at the Beards residence." I knew Mr. Scant would not elaborate, no matter how many times I asked, so did as he said. But on the way up the stairs, I paused.

"Mr. Scant?" I said, looking back down at him.

"Yes, Master Oliver?"

"I just wanted to say . . ."

"Yes, Master Oliver?"

"I . . . would like to accept your apology. For fooling me, and such."

Mr. Scant gave a smart bow. "Most gracious of you, Master Oliver. In the same spirit, I should like to remind you of your words to me: 'I'm so, so sorry . . . I couldn't do a thing because I'm completely and utterly useless.' If you would allow me, I would like to echo your sentiments and also accept that apology."

"Don't be a rotter, Mr. Scant."

Mr. Scant's lips twitched at the edges. Only a little, but that was reward enough for me.

Upstairs, Mother told me off sternly. She had finally found my brown jacket, the one with all the soot on it from the British Library. I had meant to lose it at school, but had forgotten and simply left it in my wardrobe. Mother thrust it at me and commanded me to give it to Penny, who was standing just behind her. For her part, Penny wagged a finger at me before reaching out to take the jacket, amused as ever that I was in trouble. To my relief, Mother didn't ask how the jacket had gotten into such a state.

I managed to sleep by promising myself dreams of disappearing into the sky in a hot air balloon. But once again, that wasn't how dreaming worked: instead, I had a strange one about farm animals being hung in a steeple to act as church bells, whereupon I had to pretend to play the church organ.

That said, when Mr. Scant gently woke me, I was ready for him. As though I had been awake and alert all along, I asked, "Is it time?"

"It is indeed," he whispered. "Bring winter clothes. It gets cold up there."

XIV
The Theft of a Brother

Mr. Scant's staunch ally Dr. Mikolaitis was waiting for us outside the gates, seated atop something I had certainly not expected. Not a horse-drawn carriage this time but, remarkably, a great steam traction engine, sputtering away all the predawn silence. Even in the dim light, I could see the machine was a beauty—and a familiar one. Words painted in gold lettering lined the canopy behind its chimney, and even though I couldn't quite discern them, I already knew what they spelled out: *Diplexito Engineering & Combustibles (Tunbridge Wells) Ltd.* Though I had only seen the vehicle in motion twice before, I knew it well: Father's haulage machine. Many times I had played on it as a child—while it was stationary—and rather loved the strangeness of the vehicle. The machine looked like a small train, but its large wheels were meant for roads rather than tracks. And instead of pulling a carriage, it towed a large wagon that I could only assume held the hot air balloon borrowed from Mr. Beards.

Dr. Mikolaitis had donned overalls and a cap, looking very much the part, and smoked a cigarette as we approached. "Let's go and get your brother," he said to Mr. Scant. "This weather, it freezes my spit before it hits the ground. And this beast makes far too much noise for my liking."

The doctor helped me up to the little driving space, where, with a bit of stoking and a bit of lever-pulling, he put us into motion. Progress was slow, of course, but once advancing downhill, the engine picked up some speed.

Mr. Gaunt's house was some fifteen miles away, so by the time we drew close, the sky had turned light. I assumed that Mr. Scant had planned for that. A few curious farmers watched as our traction engine passed, sending its white totem of steam up into the crisp morning air as it chugged on down the crumbly roads on the outskirts of town. Finally, Mr. Scant directed us off the road and up a mud track, leading to a large wooden gate.

"Straight through?" called Dr. Mikolaitis.

"Straight through!" Mr. Scant shouted back.

With his eyes narrowed, Dr. Mikolaitis sent the vehicle into the gate at full speed. The result was somewhat underwhelming: the heavy engine had already struggled to climb uphill, so after the front of the boiler bashed against the gates, a protracted moment of silence followed.

"Was something meant to happen?" I asked, but before anyone could answer, the wood gave way and we were through. Indeed, the gates crunched in a satisfying manner under the engine's wheels. On the other side, Mr. Scant jumped down and beckoned for me to follow, which I did, letting him catch and steady me on the muddy ground.

"Get her ready," Mr. Scant called up to Dr. Mikolaitis, with a nod back at the trailer. I felt a thrill of excitement as Dr. Mikolaitis saluted. No matter what happened today, the chance to take flight would be joy enough to make up for anything else. Then I remembered we could all end up dead, and rebuked myself for being so childish.

Breaking into Mr. Gaunt's farmhouse posed no difficulty—Mr. Scant's claw pried open a small window, and I was pushed through it. This must be how burglars went about their business, I thought as I landed. I froze as something rushed past my feet—only a small white cat, with a ribbon atop its ugly head. The creature regarded me with suspicion but soon lost interest, and I breathed a sigh of relief. Had there been a vicious guard dog instead, it would have altogether spoilt my day.

Mr. Gaunt had left the front door key on a hook just next to the lock. When I let Mr. Scant in, he moved like a vengeful ghost, surging through the house and up the stairs, a sight that prompted a troubled yowl from the cat. I followed, and when I reached a small bedroom, I saw Mr. Scant had already begun shaking his brother awake.

"No, no, no . . ." Mr. Scant's brother was saying. "Why are you so bloody *predictable?*"

The commotion had roused Mr. Gaunt's wife, who put on her glasses with a look of annoyance. "Language! What's going on?"

"Heck is being insane, as usual," replied Mr. Gaunt.

"Please pardon the intrusion, Winifred, but we have to leave now," said Mr. Scant. "You are in very grave danger."

"No, *you* are in danger," his brother answered. "Have you lost your wits?"

"Now is the time," said Mr. Scant. "We're getting away, whether you like it or not."

He reached out, but Mr. Gaunt slapped his hand away. "We are not going anywhere," Mr. Gaunt said. "This is where we're *safe*."

"You are not, and you know it. Now come, get dressed."

"Reginald, what is going on?"

"Nothing, my darling, nothing, nothing."

"Don't tell me it's that *business* come up again . . ."

"No, it's . . ."

"I thought it was all over and done with!"

Mr. Gaunt winced as his rather short wife drew herself up in her bed, as much as she could manage.

"What have you been keeping from me?"

"Winifred, please, let me speak with my brother."

"Go right on ahead, as you please! But don't expect me to hold back from sticking my oar in!"

"Heck, this is ridiculous," said Mr. Gaunt. "You know they won't stand for it. I can't go *anywhere* without them knowing."

"Of course I know."

"Well, then, why are you *here*?"

Winifred Gaunt readied one of her oars. "It *is* true!" she cried. "Isn't it? Oh, no wonder you never liked my idea to go and live in France! Have they been here, watching us all these years? What about Ellie?"

"Elspeth will be quite safe, my darling. *Please!* I need to think. She's safe as long as we're *here.*"

"Oh, you know that for sure, do you?"

Mr. Scant attempted to hold up a reassuring hand, but his mechanical claw made Mrs. Gaunt shriek.

"You brought that thing into my bedroom?" his brother barked. "You think you're going to be *fighting*?"

"Not if you *listen* to me."

"They'll come for us, and if they don't find us, they'll come for our Elspeth."

"You should know that if I'm here, I've thought of all that already."

That seemed to derail Mr. Gaunt's train of thought. He squinted at his brother's face. "You've thought it through properly?" he said. "Not . . . not some half-baked thought-about-it-in-the-bath demi-plan?"

"There's an air balloon outside waiting for us."

Mr. Gaunt held his brother's gaze, which I knew from experience was a nerve-wracking ordeal. Then he let his head drop. "A balloon, he says. Madness. Fine. Give us ten minutes to get dressed."

"Five," said Mr. Scant and beckoned me to the door with his claw.

⸙

Dr. Mikolaitis was smoking again when we found him. He had stationed himself near a barn of sorts—more a shelter for hay bales, open on three sides. The balloon was not a heartening sight, not yet even half-full. What made it inflate, I could not say, but a hose connected it to the now-detached trailer.

"Are we surrounded?" Mr. Scant asked.

"Of course," said the scarred man.

"Is it ready?"

"Ten, fifteen minutes more."

"Tricky."

"Now who's this?" said Mr. Gaunt, catching up to us.

Dr. Mikolaitis ignored him. "This hydrogen business is not quick. Perhaps I go to cause a ruckus, if you need it."

"No. We need you with us." Mr. Scant thumped his comrade on the shoulder in an encouraging sort of way.

"That's Dr. Mikolaitis," I told Mr. Gaunt, as no

⸙ 199 ⸙

one else had made the introduction. "Don't be scared by his face. He's a good man."

"I've seen you before!" Mr. Gaunt said. "You're one of—"

"Hello, Mr. Gaunt," said Dr. Mikolaitis. "Or should I call you Mr. Scant the Younger, now? You're looking well. The truth is that I am your brother's man on the inside. Ah—you are going to ask how you can know I am not the Society's man on the inside here. You must trust me. And think to yourself—would I really be here, doing what I am doing, if I am on their side?"

"Well, I suppose there's not a lot of point standing about arguing about it, is there?" said Mr. Gaunt.

Mr. Scant turned to his brother. "Where's Winifred?" he asked.

"She insisted we bring Lady Hortensia. The cat. Putting the poor creature into her handbag. She won't be—ah, there she is."

Mr. Gaunt's wife had stepped out of the house and strode toward us with purpose. I looked with pity at the brown handbag swinging from her arm.

Mr. Scant again addressed Dr. Mikolaitis. "How long?"

"Still ten minutes. Should I set off the flares?"

"Not yet. They'll catch on and start shooting into the air."

Mrs. Gaunt reached us at the barn, demanding, "Here, what have you done with our gate?"

"Knocked it down," said Mr. Scant. "Please lower your voice. We are watched."

Mrs. Gaunt's eyes widened, and she clutched her handbag tightly. It let out a faint yowl.

"What exactly is the problem?" asked Mr. Gaunt.

"We need more time to get the balloon ready. We need a distraction."

"Hmm. Could always use the horses," Mr. Gaunt said. "Get some old clothes and stuff them with straw and set the horses loose."

Dr. Mikolaitis and Mr. Scant looked at him for a few seconds, then at one another. Mr. Scant nodded.

"I'll go and grab some clothes, then," said Mr. Gaunt.

"Please hurry," said his brother.

Inside a small stable a matter of yards away, Mr. Scant found and quickly saddled three horses. Mrs. Gaunt followed him around, making a fuss but ensuring the straps were all properly fastened as she went. Mr. Gaunt appeared with some old clothes, and we all set about stuffing them with straw. The

Scant brothers then strapped the improvised manne-
quins to the horses, posed like riders bent low.

Mr. Scant led the horses to the stable door and
turned to the rest of us. "Take these flares to Dr.
Mikolaitis," he said, distributing them among us.
He stayed where he was as we stepped out, and Dr.
Mikolaitis beckoned us over. "Not a moment too
soon," he said, nodding toward the smashed gates.
A shiny black motorcar had appeared there, and two
men with greatcoats stepped out to regard us from
under the brims of bowler hats. A moment later,
a number of other men in the same coats dropped
down from the walls of Mr. Gaunt's grounds.

"Get in the basket of the balloon," said Dr. Mikolaitis, taking the flares from Mr. and Mrs. Gaunt,
who both looked happy to be rid of the things. "Boy,
stay here and help me."

Dr. Mikolaitis lit the first flare with a match, and
then the others, directing me to place two of them
a few paces away. I hurried to do as he said, and as
smoke began to spread, the men began their advance.
They were still quite some distance away, and walking with the caution of men expecting to tread on
booby traps, but they would be upon us in a minute
or less.

Dr. Mikolaitis grabbed my wrist and led me back toward the stable. Mr. Scant waited there with the horses, and once we were clear of the risk of being trampled, he set them running through the smoke in all directions. With any luck, the Society men would chase the effigies, thinking that we had tried to make our escape on horseback. As a final measure, Mr. Scant guided us through the smoke to where the steam traction engine still stood, climbed up, and set it running in the approximate direction of the motorcar.

"Good-bye, steam traction engine," said Dr. Mikolaitis, in a grand tone. "You served us well, but now we take to the skies!"

Cries of confusion began to ring out from all around us, and we hurried to join Mr. and Mrs. Gaunt in the balloon's basket. Mr. Scant helped me in amongst various boxes, cylinders, and capsules. We started to heft sandbags over the side, and Mrs. Gaunt let out a yelp as the basket lurched forward, bumping along the ground once or twice before it took to the air—narrowly missing the roof of the barn. A faint meowing emerged from Mrs. Gaunt's handbag, so she shushed it, running a hand comfortingly over its straps.

"We're going! We're going!" I cried, unable to restrain myself. I pulled the scarf back over my mouth and tried to see the ground, but there was nothing below but grayness. However, as we burst out of the smoke, I felt my legs go weak: we had ascended much higher than I had expected, and much more quickly.

"What's the matter?" Dr. Mikolaitis said as I slid down onto the floor of the basket.

"Everything's so small," I whispered. "I don't think I like flying very much after all."

"Which way are we going?" Mr. Gaunt yelled.

"It doesn't matter very much," said Mr. Scant. "The wind will take us."

"What the devil do you mean, it doesn't matter?"

"Any way is as good as the next, really. What matters is that we move the things in the basket aside when we know what direction the harpoon will come from."

"*Harpoon?*" Reginald and Winifred Gaunt cried together, in the perfect unison of two people who had been married a very long time.

"Yes," Mr. Scant said. "Any sighting?"

"Not yet," Dr. Mikolaitis said, scanning the skies with a small telescope. "Probably not for some minutes."

"Keep looking. Master Oliver, you'd best stand. You don't want to be impaled, so be sure to be quick on your feet."

The best I could do was get to my knees and peep over the edge. Eventually, I noticed the round shadow we were casting on the ground, and the sight amused me somehow. "I can see our shadow!" I said. "Come and see!"

"Not on your life!" said Mrs. Gaunt.

"It's not so scary once you're used to it," I remarked, as casually as I could. Then I noticed something else. "What's that other shadow?"

Dr. Mikolaitis leaned over me. "Ah. Upwards," he said, before going to the other side of the basket and pointing his telescope up toward the sun. "There she blows."

I didn't need a telescope of my own to see what he meant. Descending upon us, with a shadow that would soon swallow us up entirely, was an immense, dark dirigible—very much like a great sea monster swimming toward its helpless, drifting prey.

XV
Harpooned

"Clear this area here," said Mr. Scant, pushing me and his twin aside, then shifting some of the small boxes. This made the gondola hang in a slightly lopsided way, but Mr. Scant didn't seem worried. As the dirigible came closer, we made no attempt to escape. Our balloon's steering method was rudimentary—but even with state-of-the-art controls, any attempt to escape would have been futile.

The reason Mr. Scant had cleared part of the basket soon became evident. The dirigible shot several harpoons at us, and while most missed, dangling forlornly until they were wound back in, one hit. It burst through the side of the basket and then through the bottom as well, sending splinters in all directions.

The great airship did not reel us in, as I had

presumed it would. Instead, it very slowly began to turn. After a time, I realized that the ship had started propelling itself away from us: we were being towed. Dislodging the harpoon would be our only way to escape, but that would only invite the firing of another. Judging from his folded arms and the pointed way he ignored Mrs. Gaunt's stream of accusations, though, Mr. Scant was not worried. His brother stayed silent, but if Mr. Gaunt was afraid, he hid it far better than I would have expected.

Mrs. Gaunt eventually ran out of breath and sat down, then struggled to keep poor Lady Hortensia inside her handbag as she fished about for a paper fan. After some time drifting, Mr. Scant raised his voice over the hum of the dirigible's engines. "You can see the Thames. We're being taken out toward Gravesend."

"An appropriate name, maybe," muttered Dr. Mikolaitis.

Mr. Gaunt let out a heavy breath. "It's bringing us to the Cobham Mausoleum. One of *their* places."

Mr. Scant nodded, his face growing grimmer, which scarcely seemed possible. When it became clear nobody was going to explain any further, I had to speak. "Whose places? What's happening?"

"Reginald means that this mausoleum has been taken as a playground by the rich men who fancy themselves magicians," Mr. Scant said.

"*Mages*," his brother said. "They say they're mages. If we're being precise, what they're really doing is trying to convince *each other* they want to be mages. Daft. All of them quietly complain about how absurd the whole thing is, how it's all ridiculous and childish and they know it—but when they gather together en masse, not one of them will admit it."

"Do you remember my little display of legerdemain with my claw, Master Oliver?" asked Mr. Scant.

"When you turned that claw made of scraps into the real one? I remember."

"Perhaps now would be an appropriate time for some more," Mr. Scant said. He showed the palms of his white gloves—the claw still being in its bag—and then clapped them together. When he opened them, a small pencil had appeared, with strip of paper wrapped around it. After licking the lead, Mr. Scant wrote a short message. Then he looked back to me. "Magic trick number two: producing a dove."

Mr. Scant opened one of the boxes in the basket just enough to draw out a bird from within. He put the message into a tube attached to the bird's leg, while Mrs. Gaunt moved her handbag a little further away. Then Mr. Scant sent the messenger bird flapping out into the open air.

"Abracadabra!" he said.

"Glad you're enjoying yourself," said Mr. Gaunt, as Dr. Mikolaitis snorted a little laugh.

As the dark dirigible continued to pull us along like fish on a line, the two Scant brothers stood side-by-side to look for landmarks ahead of us. Soon they were teasing one another about magic tricks they had learnt as children and laughing as though they had never been apart—as though they'd both remembered they were family. Mrs. Gaunt sniffed and told Lady Hortensia how silly they were, but I could see her smiling too. The few other times I had heard Mr. Scant laugh, the sound had seemed an aberration of sorts, but now it came entirely unforced. For a moment, in the middle of the sky, I witnessed an affectionate normalcy return to two men's very strange lives.

Dr. Mikolaitis was standing alone, so I went to his side. "Not afraid to look any longer?" he asked.

I peered out of the basket. "We're a lot lower now."

"Yes. Slowly, we are descending. Does it make you less afraid, like this?"

"I suppose it wouldn't make any difference—falling out from here, compared with falling out when we were higher."

He stuck his bottom lip out thoughtfully. "Maybe you have a few seconds fewer for enjoying the view."

"There is that."

"Look, you can see the mausoleum now—there, you see it?"

"Where?"

"There."

The winter mist had made a bumpy gray quilt of the countryside, but after a few moments, I found the particular piece of gray Dr. Mikolaitis was showing me: a large square building with columns all about it, set in a circle of stone, with a pyramid for its roof. More on the scale of a townhouse than a palace or a museum, the Cobham Mausoleum nevertheless stood grandiose and forbidding from its lonely place on a hill, amongst skeletal, winter-stripped trees.

"They call it a mausoleum, but no one has ever been laid to rest there," Dr. Mikolaitis said. He had produced another cigarette and already looked bored with smoking it. "Possibly it was always built as a place of magicks. The earl who lives, ah . . . hereabouts, he owns this place. But once the Lice showed an interest, he wanted no more to do with it."

"What do you suppose they will do to us?"

"Oh, I would not like to guess at this. Perhaps their rituals are in need of body parts for magic spells—I imagine young ones are the best kind." His cigarette flared for a moment before he hungrily sucked down the smoke. "But you know, I would not worry too much."

"Well, that certainly sets me at ease," I said.

Dr. Mikolaitis grinned. "You remind me of myself as a boy. You want to sound brave, so you make a joke. It makes it sound like you are not afraid."

"I'm not a coward!"

"No. I do not think that you are." Stubbing out his cigarette on the corner of a wooden box, he produced a toothpick to worry at his teeth. "But only a madman is afraid of nothing. It is the man who accepts his fear and still acts who is brave. But to laugh at fear to hide it away is a means to fool other people. As a coward would."

I didn't know what to say to that, so I nodded slowly. Dr. Mikolaitis took that as the end of our conversation and flicked his toothpick over the edge of the basket. By then, the dirigible had pulled us close enough to the ground that Mr. Scant said we ought to get to the business of deflating the balloon.

"The man in charge will want to drag the whole thing inside the building," Mr. Scant added. "That's his way. We must be sure that he gets it."

"You know who's in charge, I assume," said Mr. Gaunt.

"I do."

The dirigible landed first, and from inside its large gondola came none other than the Valkyrie. She stalked over to us with a cheery cry of "Special service!" and sliced the rope attaching us to the dirigible with her cleaver. "Whoopsie!" she cooed, grabbing the rope before we could drift away. With that in hand, she hauled our hovering basket, and us within it, to the doors of the mausoleum. Once we were close enough, the Valkyrie hauled us through the doors and cut away the ropes that attached the basket to the balloon, sending us crashing to the floor. That left me, Mr. Scant, and the rest of our party rather absurdly gathered in a little basket inside the grand mausoleum.

Though this tomb was empty of the dead, the living had gathered around us. Mysterious figures in monks' habits stood with their faces hidden in shadow. A multitude of candles had been laid out in intricate patterns and strange circles drawn on the floors. From the pillars, grotesques leered down at us with their ugly faces.

"I don't like this one bit," Mrs. Gaunt said, clinging tight to her husband. I wouldn't have minded Mother or even Father being there for me to cling to, but I stood alone, wanting to look brave. Not merely to look brave, but to *be* brave.

And then one of the men stepped forward and pulled down his hood. In my shock, I actually pointed my finger and cried out, "It's you!"

So unexpected was the sight that I couldn't help myself. I had to state the obvious.

"You're Mr. Binns!"

XVI

Inside the Mausoleum

Mr. Binns had no time for me. Instead, he pointed at Mr. Gaunt and barked, "Gaunt! You traitor!"

Mr. Gaunt gripped the edge of the basket. "My name is Gaunt now, but I was born a Scant. This is my brother!"

"*Argh!*" A frustrated Mr. Binns reached up as if to tear his hair out. "You've just lost me another five pounds."

Another figure stepped forward and lowered her hood: Mrs. Binns, wearing a satisfied smirk. "Another win for me. So obvious, when Gaunt made a fuss about going to the Diplexito house. I'll make a note of it in the book."

Mr. Binns preferred yelling at us to acknowledging his wife. "And here's the Diplexito boy! And

Mrs. Gaunt! And even Dr. Mikolaitis. Oh, you Russian turncoat!"

"Lithuanian," Dr. Mikolaitis replied.

"Ah, Gaunt, Gaunt. I knew you were dishonest, Gaunt. I gave you everything you asked for, and this is how you repay me? And you, the ever-infuriating Claw! Burning that pathetic burrow of yours wasn't enough, eh? You should have run while you had the chance. Always the gentleman, weren't you, Scant? There by Sandleforth's side, watching me, waiting to steal away my property."

"My brother is not your property," Mr. Scant said.

"Oh, but he is! Isn't he, Thomasina?"

"He is," said Mrs. Binns, smiling very sweetly. "He made a blood pledge."

Mr. Binns laughed. "And you thought you could run away in one of my company's balloons. You weren't expecting us to give chase in the *Indefatigable* herself, though, were you now? *That* put a stop to your little adventure. Oh, the Claw. The Claw, the Claw. You've been a real thorn in my side these past months. Every time I reclaimed one of the order's relics, you stole it from us."

"Their importance to you was clear from how long you waited to sell them on."

"Well, we must maintain relations with our brothers in the East," Mr. Binns said. "Your actions were bad for business. Did you really think it wise to damage our standing as the world's foremost hidden mystical society?"

I thought I heard Dr. Mikolaitis stifle a laugh.

"Nothing I returned ever belonged to you," Mr. Scant said. "Not a thing. Nor does my brother. I am taking him back. He will have no more part in your petty burglaries."

"Burglaries, he says!" Mr. Binns pantomimed shock. "When we are only reclaiming what is ours."

His wife nodded. "You know nothing of the truth of this world," she said, stepping toward our basket with eyes like a snake's and a grin like a jackal's. "The artifacts of the great men who founded this order should be with those who . . . best appreciate them. And you. What are you doing here, little Oliver?" she asked. "The young accomplice we heard so much about—could that really have been you?"

When I didn't answer, her look soured.

"I asked you a question."

"What you are doing is wrong!" I shouted.

"It was him! I can see it in his eyes, my darling. Ah! If only we'd had a wager on that," Mrs. Binns said, turning away sharply. "The problem with children is they repeat what their parents and priests tell them and imagine that means they know right from wrong!"

"He's young," said Mr. Binns. "He doesn't know we decide such things. We who have the power in this world."

Thomasina Binns looked back at me as though I were something she had found on her shoe. "Scant, it was cruel of you to bring a child here. You must have understood that our friends in the East would pay very well for a sweet, angel-faced young servant boy."

"Master Oliver is under my protection."

"For all the use *that* is!" snapped Mr. Binns.

His wife sneered. "You are still failing to understand your situation. Valkyrie!"

Like an iceberg on a dark sea, the Valkyrie loomed behind us. "Madam?"

"Bring the boy to me."

In a single motion, Mr. Scant pushed me behind him and raised the claw, three blades pointed at the Valkyrie's eyes and throat. She hesitated, but Mr. Binns laughed and gave a little delighted clap.

"And there it is, the famous claw!" From within his jacket, he produced an ornate dueling pistol. His wife drew out a matching one from somewhere behind her back, and the two of them gave each other a soppy sort of look as they cocked the hammers.

"I want it," Mr. Binns said, leveling his weapon.

"Very splendid pistols," Mr. Scant said. "Made by Mr. Joseph Egg himself, by the look of it. Why would you need my lowly claw when you have such fine weapons?"

"New toys are always the most desirable," said Mr. Binns.

"Particularly when they belong to someone else," added his wife. "Now take it off and hand it over."

Though I was certain Mr. Scant would fight, he made no move. Then, to my dismay, he undid the strap at his wrist and tossed the claw to Mr. Binns.

"What are you *doing?*" I cried, but Mr. Scant's face may as well have been made of the same Portland stone as the walls.

With a look of satisfaction, Mr. Binns picked up the discarded claw—gingerly, as one might pick up a scorpion. When it became apparent the claw would deliver no hidden sting, he grinned like a maniac and pulled it on, handing his pistol to his wife. He marveled at the device for a few moments, cycling his fingers once or twice to see how the digits moved, then lowered one finger until it fixed on me.

"Now," he said. "Bring m—"

But that was as far as he got, because Mr. Scant bellowed, "*Now!*"

Dr. Mikolaitis pulled on a cord, and with a great flash of light, one side of the basket fell away while a plume of smoke gushed out. A moment later, a number of small fireworks screeched in every direction like mad bats, while Dr. Mikolaitis and Mr. Scant dashed forward, slinging knives at the pistols Mrs. Binns was pointing at them. Dr. Mikolaitis' knife hit the gun in her left hand squarely, but Mr. Scant's hit her on her right hand itself. She let out a terrible scream, firing the pistol into the air.

"Bad show!" I heard Dr. Mikolaitis shout.

"I'm hopeless with those things and you know it!" Mr. Scant snapped back. He turned to deal with the Valkyrie, swinging his claw up to catch her cleaver before it split his skull—not the claw worn by Mr. Binns but the one made of scraps from the ruins of the Ice House.

Someone was pulling my shoulder. I looked back to see Mr. Gaunt yelling something, and though I could not make out the words, he clearly wanted us to leave. This seemed like a good idea.

Mr. Scant may not have liked knives, but he was in his element with a claw, even one made of charred engine parts and ruined laboratory equipment. He once more deflected one of the Valkyrie's cleavers, forcing her back, then ran up the harpoon stuck fast into the basket and vaulted over the giant woman's shoulder. On the way down, he kicked the back of her leg so hard that she collapsed. Dr. Mikolaitis kept the other men in cloaks at bay with his knives, while Mrs. Gaunt sprinted toward the door. She went at an incredible speed despite her skirts, with her fingers straight like an athlete's and her long-suffering hand-bag swinging wildly from her shoulder.

Mr. Binns had recovered one of the guns his wife had dropped and attempted to shoot Dr. Miko-laitis, but the throwing knife had jammed something inside the barrel. Dr. Mikolaitis jumped up to kick Mr. Binns square in the jaw, while Mr. Scant jumped back to prevent the Valkyrie grabbing his ankle. As Mr. Binns went sprawling, he knocked over a cande-labra and one of the mystical drapes caught fire.

As I watched, the fire quickly ate up the thin fabric, and spread to the cloak of one of the silent observers. The man commenced awkwardly trying to stamp the flames out without disrobing, while others around him tried to help. Just then, Mr. Scant appeared by my side, urging me to run, and moments later, we were at the door—then through it, starting down the steps. The flashes of the fireworks were nothing compared to the brightness of the day, and my eyes took a few seconds to adjust. This could be called a small blessing, I suppose: for a few peaceful moments, I couldn't see the crowd of robed men with spears who had encircled the mausoleum. We were surrounded.

XVII
A Stern Talking-To

Scant was not cowed by the sight of a few spears. He had a claw made of bits and pieces of scrap metal, and that was more than enough for him.

"Make for the dirigible," he said. "But do *not* get on board."

He led the charge, and I followed, trying to help his brother along as the ailing Mr. Gaunt wheezed and stumbled. Mrs. Gaunt had taken to shouting obscenities at anyone who approached, and Dr. Mikolaitis kept pace behind us, watching for the Valkyrie. The act of cutting through the circle wasn't as difficult as I had expected, as the men fell over one another to keep away from Mr. Scant, only resuming their brave poses when we had already passed. Dr. Mikolaitis only had one knife left, but people still dived as he raised it toward them.

The real threat came from the Valkyrie, who had appeared from the mausoleum and was in pursuit. As we closed in on the dirigible, Mr. Scant drew us in another direction, straight past the *Indefatigable*.

"For pity's sake, where are we *going*?" Mrs. Gaunt demanded.

"Just wait," said Mr. Scant.

"Wait for what?"

"For *whom*," Mr. Scant said, before charging down three of the spear-bearing men. Grappling with them held Mr. Scant up for long enough that Dr. Mikolaitis was forced to contend with the Valkyrie. He drew out a bomb from somewhere in his waistcoat, lit the percussion fuse with his cigarette, and hurled it at her with a battle cry in his native tongue. The Valkyrie judged the length of the fuse and fearlessly kicked the bomb away, not even looking at it as it exploded. The distraction allowed us to get farther from her, but more hooded men were appearing from the trees and Mr. Gaunt had grown exhausted.

"Heck . . ." I heard Dr. Mikolaitis breathe.

"I know," said Mr. Scant, holding out his hands to gather us behind him.

"Reggie can't go on!" wailed Mrs. Gaunt. "It's the end!"

Dr. Mikolaitis threw his last knife at the nearest group of men, hitting someone in the leg. Then he lit another cigarette and said, "Better get ready for a last stand."

I looked to Mr. Scant. "Last stand?"

Mr. Gaunt laughed grimly. "Three men, one woman, a child, and a cat in a handbag," he said, between labored breaths. "Don't fancy our chances."

"Mr. Scant, there's a plan, isn't there?" I asked.

"There's a hope."

"I've fought my way out of worse," Dr. Mikolaitis said, positioning himself between Mr. and Mrs. Gaunt and the Valkyrie. "My friend, it's been a pleasure."

"As always, Mykolas," said Mr. Scant.

The Valkyrie hit her cleavers together hard enough that sparks flew out. Mr. Scant was not looking at her, however.

"Ah, perhaps it won't be necessary," he said. "Can you hear that? It seems our timing wasn't so bad after all."

I pricked up my ears. Under the percussion of the Valkyrie's cleavers was the steady basso continuo of a motor engine.

"He's here!" said Mr. Scant.

"Who's here?" his brother asked.

"My employer. My friend. My master."

From the trail leading through the trees sped an emerald-green motorcar with a windshield and solid roof. I knew it at once: Father's Hylas Green Knight, with a Diplexito engine. I called out to him in delight again and again.

The motorcar careened in our direction, sending hooded men scattering, and then from the passenger-side window erupted the whiskers and jowls of my very own father. With a disgruntled look, he raised the old blunderbuss he kept behind his desk and took aim at the Valkyrie. She and the men around her dived for cover as the old gun's report filled the sky. The car came to a halt only a few paces from where we stood.

"Scant! What in the blazes is all this, and who are these bounders?" roared Father.

"Lawless hoodlums, sir," said Mr. Scant, already opening the back door and ushering us in. "You know the sort."

"I know the sort," said Father.

I sat sandwiched in the Green Knight between Mr. and Mrs. Gaunt, while to add another level to my already towering astonishment, Mrs. George turned from the driving seat to give me a wink. "Hello, Duck," she said.

Mr. Scant had dashed over to stand outside of the driver's side door. Dr. Mikolaitis, meanwhile, clung to the back of the vehicle. Mr. Scant leaned in and said, "Drive, Mrs. George, drive!" Only a moment later, when we were in motion, did he ask, "Why is Mrs. George driving?"

"You weren't there to grab the wheel, were you, Scant?" Father answered. "And I wasn't about to send for Williams just because of some harebrained message from a pigeon's leg. So Mrs. George said she was capable and I said, 'Why not?'"

"Poop-poop!" said Mrs. George, bright-eyed. She didn't even need to raise her voice to be heard over the engine. "You said it were an emergency, so we decided there weren't no time to muck about."

"Too right!" said Father. "Turn us around and let's get out of here. Now what's all this hullabaloo about? Were they going to harm the boy? Boy! Are you quite all right?"

"I am," I said.

"Hmm," said Father. "Was he *really* in any danger?"

I wondered if Father had expected a blubbering mess. "I certainly was!" I said.

From his place outside the door, Mr. Scant replied, "No doubt about it, sir. The threats were very clear."

"Hmm. Well, can't let the bounders get away with that, now, can we?" Father said, leaning out of the window to take another shot. When he reappeared, he gave me a nod and said, "You're safe now, boy. Father's here to fix everything."

"Thank you, Father," I managed. This was about the kindest thing he had ever done for me, and yet I felt no joy from hearing it.

"Erm . . . someone's getting in our way up ahead," said Mrs. George. As if to confirm, Dr. Mikolaitis banged on the roof. Mrs. George's efforts to turn the motorcar had taken us closer to the mausoleum; we were now back where the Green Knight had first appeared. And there stood the Valkyrie, looking for all the world like a bull about to charge.

"She'll soon get out of the way, I think," said Father.

"She won't," I said. "You don't know her, Father."

"Ramming speed, then."

"With this great lot of us, she doesn't go much faster, sir!" said Mrs. George.

"Give it everything she's got."

"She might actually stop us, sir," Mr. Scant remarked.

"Nonsense! You really think so?"

"I think that all might be lost if she *does*, sir."

"She's strong as a gorilla!" I put in.

"Son, there's a Diplexito engine in this beauty! Not a one has been stopped by a gorilla before!" With that, Father squeezed the horn, and in a voice liable to drown it out, bellowed, "Full steam ahead!"

"Lord have mercy!" cried Mrs. Gaunt. The small space I had grew smaller still as she squirmed about beside me, making the sign of the cross. As we moved closer and closer, the Valkyrie braced herself—and then jumped.

With a great thump, she landed in front of the windscreen. "She jumped on the car, the blimmin' loon!" Mrs. George yelled. "Look at this!"

"Keep going!" Mr. Scant urged her.

"We're going! We're going!"

"I'll get her off!" Father declared, leaning out of the window again. A moment later, he looked back to us, wide-eyed. "She got my arm! By God, that's a grip like a vice. What are you, a lobster in skirts?"

From my place in the back, I could hear Mr. Scant climb up onto the roof, but the Valkyrie now sat astride the front of the motorcar, brandishing a cleaver in the hand free of Father's arm. "One false move and I chop off his arm!" she shouted up at Mr. Scant.

"Hold on a minute . . ." Mrs. George said, squinting through the windscreen. "Right, I'll sort this out."

"What are you doing?" Mr. Gaunt yelped, as Mrs. George brought the car to a stop. I shook my head as she opened the door, but to no avail. Father fumbled with his blunderbuss, one-handed, but there was no way he could reload it while in the Valkyrie's grip.

"I've had enough of this," said Mrs. George, getting out of the car. "And when I say enough's enough, it is *enough*."

"We'll do something," I said. "Don't worry, Father."

Father nodded but started to breathe heavily through his whiskers as the Valkyrie raised her cleaver.

"Good choice," the Valkyrie was saying, as she climbed down from the motorcar, keeping a tight grip on Father's arm. "Now Claw, get in and drive us back to the lords and ladies, will you? It'll be short an arm or two if you're not careful."

But Mrs. George hadn't stepped out of the driver's seat to let Mr. Scant take her place. Instead, she set herself solidly in front of the much larger woman. Our dear cook was not tall, the top of her head not even level with the Valkyrie's shoulders, but she was almost as thick about the arms.

"I know you."

"I . . . What?" said the Valkyrie.

"You're Ethel's girl Tilly, aren'tcha? I remember you rolling down the hill with the Davis boys when you was only little. I'm not wrong, am I? You're the spitting image of your mam! How is Ethel these days? Not seen her since the vegetable contest at the Cuckoo Festival."

"Mam's . . . doing all right."

"And look at you! Wearing that silly plate of armor under your apron! And is that one o' yer pa's cleavers?"

"It's my own."

"Oh! So you still working in the shop too?"

"On and off . . ."

"Well, if you've got a steady trade, what you doing with that lot? Come over here and let me have a proper look at you."

Color returned to Father's face as the Valkyrie

released him. Scarcely believing my ears, I chanced a look back at Mr. Scant and Dr. Mikolaitis, who were keeping the hooded men at bay. They had already laid two of the Society men on the ground, while the other four had drawn dueling sabers.

Mrs. George continued to chide the Valkyrie. "And what are you *thinking*, jumping on our motorcar like that? I couldn't see! I might've driven straight off a cliff, and it would've been *you* we landed on. Did you not think of that?"

"No cliffs around here, Ma'am."

"Oh, you call me Mrs. George. Yer mam and pa, they're good people. You know that, don't you? I shouldn't wonder they'd be very surprised to hear about you carrying on like this. Wouldn't they?"

"They would, M-M-Miss George."

"They would."

Behind us, Dr. Mikolaitis had picked up a dropped spear and swung it viciously at the Society men, and Mr. Scant knew just when to duck to avoid being hit. The haft knocked one man so hard he bashed into another and they both collapsed to the ground. One of the makeshift claw blades had fallen from Mr. Scant's glove, and he used it to nail another Society thug to a tree by the hood of his cloak. The last attacker appeared undeterred, however, whirling his sword with expertise.

Meanwhile, Mrs. George's invective had reached its gentle climax. "Now you go on back home, and we'll be doing the same. Send my best wishes to Ethel and Jimmy. No more of this nonsense, you hear? Or you'll see the business end of my rolling pin!"

With that, Mrs. George stepped back in the motorcar and set it in motion. The Valkyrie looked as though her brain had stopped functioning—she stood blinking at empty space. Though the last Society man had been capably dueling Mr. Scant, he failed to notice Dr. Mikolaitis sneak up behind him, and was quickly incapacitated. The moment they were sure we were safe, the two men ran back to jump onto the car.

"We lost too much time," Mr. Scant said, leaning inside. "We'll be caught."

"Those men in cloaks?" Father asked.

"Their masters. They have vehicles of their own."

"Lice incoming!" Dr. Mikolaitis cried from behind us.

"Who the devil are you on about?" Father said.

"Mrs. George, we need to stop!" shouted Mr. Scant.

"But we're only just getting up to speed!"

"*Stop now!*"

"Look out!" Mrs. Gaunt cried, pointing to something down the slope to our left. Both brothers reached as one for the wheel, Mr. Gaunt from beside me and Mr. Scant from outside the window. Just as they seized it, something smashed through a nearby tree with the force of a giant's hammer. An immense and shadowy machine had rolled up the slope to the left of the road and burst out in front of us, like a great ship cresting a wave. The motorcar turned just in time to avoid it, but the terrible machine settled in front of us, entirely blocking the road home.

Our motorcar shuddered to a halt. We had been on course to collide with a tree, stopping solely thanks to a sharp incline, but only Mrs. George seemed to care. All other eyes were fixed on the monstrosity that had almost rammed us, and the large, conspicuous gun mounted on top of it.

XVIII
Motorcar and Ironclad

"**B**low me down . . ." Father breathed.

"Traction engines, dirigibles, motor-cars . . . *now* what?" Mr. Gaunt said.

The black metal thing released an ear-splitting hiss, plumes of steam escaping from around its numerous wheels, encircled by long belts that had left great gouges in the vehicle's wake.

"What is it, Father?" I asked.

Father's answer sounded more like he was talking to himself. "Those are Diplock's chain wheels. They're not meant to be out of the workshop yet . . . And Foster's metalwork, or not far off . . ."

"We're dead," contributed Mr. Gaunt.

"Father, *what is it?*"

"It's a motor war car," Mrs. Gaunt said, her voice trembling. "I saw one at the Crystal Palace."

"This is worse than that," said Mr. Scant.

"Yes, especially since it's bally *working*, rather than falling to bits!" Father bellowed. "What you have before you, my son, is a *land ironclad*. Far better fortified than a war car, and about thrice the size. They obviously liked the idea of the Maxim gun on top, though. Scant, what lunatics built this?"

"I fear it was your good friends in the dirigibles business."

A hatch opened on the top of the vehicle. A furious-looking Mr. Binns emerged and took up a place behind the gun turret. His wife followed, climbing onto the ironclad's deck using a carbine like a walking stick. On her right hand, she wore Mr. Scant's claw.

"Out of the motorcar, all of you!" Mrs. Binns commanded, raising the barrel of her gun.

"Mrs. George, get the car running again," murmured Father.

"It's not going," she whispered back. "It needs starting again at the front, and I think it's overheated."

"I'll take a look," said Mr. Gaunt. "But I can't if I'm being shot."

"Let me worry about that," Father said, and opened the door. "The moment you get the chance, get moving. Son—stay with Scant. I'll sort all this out. No crying!"

"Wait!" I said. "You can't!"

Father ignored me and began to yell, "Right, you horrible—" but I grabbed his arm.

"Father! Listen to me! You can't solve everything by shouting at it. Please! That is not your friend Mr. Binns out there. He's dangerous. Listen to me! I am more than some hostage here. We've been dealing with these people for weeks. I have a plan, so please, listen to me!"

Father turned back to me, frowning. It had been a long time since I had actually looked into his eyes. They were green, like mine, which I don't think I would have been able to say with certainty until right then. His lips moved as though he was thinking things through, and then he shook his head. "Nonsense!"

Mrs. Binns was getting impatient. She pointed her carbine at Mr. Scant, who had remained outside with Dr. Mikolaitis. "Come out or I kill your beloved valet," she called to Father.

Father pulled away from me and heaved himself through the door, clutching his ridiculous old blunderbuss.

"You don't need the gun," Mr. Binns called.

"I rather think I do," Father said, pointing it up at Thomasina Binns. Mrs. Binns did not flinch. Instead, she gave a long-suffering sigh and she cleared her throat.

"My husband and I are busy people, Sandleforth. We are not like you, content to slave away to feed a dying empire. We know what is coming, and we have revolutions to plan."

"Then I should think the best thing would be for us to go on our way, don't you?" said Father.

Mr. Scant was close enough to lean through the driver's side window. "Let's not waste this opportunity."

"Heck—that's a Maxim gun," Mr. Gaunt said, easing open the passenger door on his side of the motorcar.

"You need to come with me," Mr. Scant told his brother. "I'll get the engine running faster with you."

Mr. Binns had taken up his wife's monologue. "The world is a smaller and smaller place, thanks to airships like mine. New powers are rising in the East. I can't afford to look weak in front of my colleagues, especially when I am this close to being made a *hong-men*. We hadn't planned to chase you runaway mice in our iron chariot, but then again—seizing control of rather a useful British engineering company wasn't part of our original plan either. Now put down that relic, Sandleforth, and let's talk business. Maybe I'll let you stay on as a figurehead."

"You tell that wife of yours to put her carbine down first," Father said. "And then you step away from the Maxim."

"Sandleforth, put down your weapon or I shall shoot you in the knee. Or maybe I should get your boy to help me persuade you?"

Father did not flinch at this. "You shoot me in the leg, and I will shoot back from wherever I fall. I've been shot before—have you, Roland? I know what to expect. And if I shoot back at you with this old girl, I may not hit your knee, but I will probably hit your chest and your head and a few other places. She does that. And then I suppose whichever one of us is still alive would have to start thinking about how to crawl back home. As for my boy, you jumped-up little gonoph, you go near him and I won't even need to tear your head off, because he'll do it twice before I even get started! You think I haven't had my eye on you for the last ten years? You think I don't know about your pathetic little magic club? Secret society *this* and controlling the world *that*—all nonsense spewed by weak men who don't have the gumption to claw their way to the top the old-fashioned way!"

Mr. Binns looked to his wife and said, "Thomasina, my darling—did you hear him call me a name?"

Mrs. Binns grinned. "He fancies himself such a big man. He thinks if we want him alive, he's safe. How does the poem go? 'Whatever happens, we have got the Maxim gun, and they have not.' Fire away, my dear."

"No!" I yelled. Knowing at once what I had to do, I dashed out from behind the motorcar and skidded to a halt in front of Father with my arms spread.

"What a brave boy," cooed Mrs. Binns. "A shame we don't need him."

A few moments later, the Maxim gun began to whir. I felt Father's hand grab my arm and haul me backwards, but someone else had appeared, half-dashing and half-falling to get in front of me. It was Mr. Gaunt, who had grabbed Father's blunderbuss.

For a moment, everything was still. Mr. Binns froze in fear before he could aim the barrel of the Maxim gun at Mr. Gaunt. Mrs. Binns stepped toward her husband, wide eyed. But Mr. Gaunt had no reason to hesitate. He squeezed the trigger.

And then, after a click, nothing happened. Father had been bluffing; he'd never reloaded the weapon.

A look of unbridled wrath crossed Mr. Binns's face. Mr. Gaunt had sincerely attempted to kill him but had failed. And that made Mr. Binns very, very angry. The whir began again.

Ruefully, Mr. Gaunt looked back, first at me, then to his wife still in the car. He had just enough time to speak. "We must keep a stiff upper lip about these things," he said.

The big gun began spitting out little pellets eager to bite into our bodies and stop our hearts. But the stream of bullets did not tear Mr. Gaunt apart: Mrs. Binns had grabbed her husband's arm just as the gun began to fire, so the line of bullets passed close to my leg and then across the front of the motorcar.

"*Horses!*" cried Mrs. Binns. "That way, you fool!"

I saw them then—two horses coming up the incline at full gallop. Mr. Binns struggled to turn the Maxim gun while Mrs. Binns raised her carbine and fired, the report itself so loud as to slap against my skin. One horse let out a squeal, rearing up as the gun barked out. A figure leapt from its back, right up onto the ironclad. The riders were a blur of skirts and long, black hair, but I had no doubt—they were the young women I had seen riding through town with their opera glasses.

Mr. Gaunt fell to his knees, and I scarcely managed to prevent him from slumping to the ground. I struggled for a moment to keep him upright before looking back at Father, who was gawping like a fish. "Don't just sit there!" I yelled. "Help me!"

Father took a moment to react, then hurried to assist me as I tucked myself under Mr. Gaunt's arm and pulled him back toward the motorcar. "Yours, I think," Mr. Gaunt said weakly, as he held up Father's blunderbuss.

"Mr. Gaunt—are you hurt?" I asked as we opened the door of the motorcar and heaved him into the seat. "Were you shot?"

Mr. Gaunt patted himself down, looking at his hands as though expecting to see blood. "Only the once, then," he told me. "In my leg."

"Must hurt like the dickens," Father said. "Let me see, then I'll give you something stiff to drink."

"No need, I think," Mr. Gaunt said. He rapped on his lower leg with his knuckle, which gave a strangely solid sound, then rolled up his trouser leg to display an artificial foot. "See, there's the bullet!" he remarked, pointing to the little black thing that had bitten into his wooden shin. "My lucky day."

"Good show!" Father roared. I gave him an angry shove, and he looked at me in astonishment.

"Your ridiculous gun wasn't even loaded!" I cried.

Father looked affronted. "It takes a long while to get the old girl ready again. I thought a solid talking-to would be all that coward Binns needed."

"You nearly got Mr. Gaunt killed! I warned you, Father! You can't win everything by having the loudest voice! Sometimes you need to *think*."

Father just harrumphed.

"Reload that ridiculous gun of yours," I said, "and watch how we do it."

The two strange riders had advanced along the ironclad, but Mr. and Mrs. Binns were armed and capable of defending themselves. Mr. Binns lay on his back, struggling with one of the women, while Mrs. Binns swung her carbine like a club while stamping one foot on the ironclad deck. Her opponent closed in on her with an easy, fluid grace, unencumbered by her hunting skirt and riding boots.

Now that the riders had put away their opera glasses, I could at last see their faces: the two women couldn't have been more than seventeen or eighteen years old. The one fighting Mrs. Binns was the black-haired girl who had waved at me in the snow—a visitor from China, or one of its neighboring countries at the very least. The smile she had flashed during her last appearance had vanished, and with a fierce expression, she seized Mrs. Binns's carbine. Mrs. Binns snarled and stamped her heel on the deck once again. For a moment, I thought it was out of frustration, but then I understood.

"There's someone else inside the ironclad!" I yelled. Just then, the vehicle lurched, upsetting the dark-haired woman's balance.

My voice had brought Mr. Scant running to my side. "Bryony is getting the engine going again," he told me. When I looked bewildered, he clarified, "*Mrs. George.*" I had never even considered she might have any other name. Mr. Scant then checked on his brother, asking for help with the motorcar.

The sudden movement of the land ironclad had turned the tables. Mr. Binns had risen to his feet and was now restraining one of the riders, pulling one arm up behind her back. The other woman continued to struggle with Mrs. Binns for the carbine, having to duck and dodge the claws that slashed and jabbed at her. Then, through the hatch came another figure, a barrel-chested Chinese man with a big knife.

"We have to help them," I said, and Mr. Scant nodded.

"Mykolas, get me up onto that thing!" he said.

"Just shoot the scoundrels!" came a shrill voice, and I realized Mrs. Gaunt had come up behind us, with Father at her side.

"The old girl isn't ready to fire," Father said.

In exasperation, Mr. Scant began to run toward the ironclad, while the man with the knife grew closer and closer to the girl Mr. Binns was restraining.

"He'll never make it in time!" I said.

"Right! Gimme that!" I heard Mrs. Gaunt say. A moment later, a dark brown blur sailed through the air above my head. I first thought that she had thrown the blunderbuss, but in fact it was her husband's artificial foot. It hit the shoulder of the man with the knife, distracting him long enough for Mr. Scant to scale the tracks of the ironclad. He struck the larger man in the neck in a way that left him wilting like a dead flower. Mr. Binns tried to put his hostage between himself and Mr. Scant, but the young woman used the moment to switch her footing and flipped Mr. Binns clean over her shoulder. I could bear it no longer, and—ignoring Father's call—ran forward too.

"Above! *Look up!*" Mr. Scant yelled at the riders, but the two strange women heard him too late. He alone had noticed the small Beards-and-Binns airship that had emerged to drop a long yellow rope, and from Mr. Scant's expression, it was clear this was not something he had been hoping for. Mrs. Binns saw the chance of making her escape, and relinquished the carbine to jump for the rope, using the turret of the Maxim gun to reach the bottom knot. Then all at once, the muscular Chinese man, Mr. Binns, Mr. Scant, and the black-haired woman leapt at the rope. The other rider tackled Mr. Binns, and with a cry of despair for his wife, he fell short. The Chinese man managed to grab the rope with one hand, and grunted as Mr. Scant and the black-haired young woman each took hold of one of his legs.

The added weight began to drag the small airship downwards, which made Mrs. Binns extremely unhappy. She began to kick at the Chinese man's face with her fine leather boots. He lost his grip and fell, taking the black-haired young woman with him, but Mr. Scant had been ruthless in his climbing. He was able to jump from the man's shoulders to catch hold of the rope again.

Mrs. Binns gave a cry of anger and tried to kick at Scant, too, but he could deflect her blows with his false claw. Still in possession of the real one, she attempted to saw at the rope with all the blades at once, but she didn't know how to make the claw cut. In a rage, Mrs. Binns pulled the glove off her hand and threw it at Mr. Scant's face. Mr. Scant barely needed to move his head to avoid it, but Mrs. Binns's hand was now free to pull out a small pistol from around her ankle. Rather than pointing it at Mr. Scant, however, she aimed directly at the rope—if she pulled the trigger, Mr. Scant would fall.

The wind changed, unraveling Mr. Scant's scarf, and in that moment, Mrs. Binns saw the truth. I, too, had followed Mr. Scant up the rope, climbing the ironclad in time to jump with the rest, hanging onto Mr. Scant's waist as he climbed. And that was not all. Having seen the claw drop, I had caught it and pulled the glove onto my own hand.

Mr. Scant gave a great roar and heaved me upwards with all his strength.

I rose up in the air above Mrs. Binns, whose eye caught mine just as she cut the rope with a round from her pistol. Mr. Scant's claw was on my hand now, and with great satisfaction, I pressed my thumb to the little button on the side that brought out the true blades. I swiped at the rope, well above where Mrs. Binns had aimed her pistol, higher still than the part she gripped. So sharp were the claw's blades that I barely felt them cut through the rope, and for a moment, the three of us hung suspended, as if we were painted figures in some heavenly scene. And then, wax wings all melted, we began to plummet.

Dr. Mikolaitis and Father caught Mr. Scant as he fell and set him straight in a flash. Mr. Scant and Father then managed to grab Mrs. Binns and hand her over to the taller of the two young riders, while Dr. Mikolaitis caught me with a sound like "Hupla!" Dr. Mikolaitis gave me a congratulatory pat on the chest and said, "Good job!"

As the taller woman began to bind Mrs. Binns's hands, the other rider brought Mr. Binns and the muscular Chinese man down from the ironclad. There was another man behind them I hadn't seen before, also apparently from China, who I guessed had been at the controls of the land ironclad.

There was something fascinating about both young riders. The Chinese girl had sharp, intelligent eyes and a mouth quick to curl into a satisfied smirk. The other, presumably British, girl tied her knots with a machine-like efficiency, and beneath her ruler-straight fringe of brown hair was a completely impassive expression: she almost looked bored.

With a wheeze and a sputter, the motorcar returned to life. "There! It's working! *Gah!*" said Mr. Gaunt. His artificial leg back in place, he had been cranking the engine until he turned around to see the young women in riding dresses clearly for the first time. Winifred Gaunt, at her husband's side, had covered her mouth with both hands.

"Ellie!" Mr. Gaunt exclaimed.

"Hello, Father," said Elspeth Gaunt.

"But what are you doing here? You should be in Paris."

"And yet I'm here in England," said Miss Gaunt. "I have been for a week. We had to catch these Tri-Loom criminals."

"Wuh . . . Wah . . . *Why?*" her mother managed.

"I am helping Cai Zhao-Ji." She gestured to the other rider, who stopped rubbing her sore arm to bow. "This is Cai Zhao-Ji."

"Your daughter is a wonderful person," said Cai Zhao-Ji, with only a hint of an accent. "Please don't worry—we know how to keep her safe. She was a target of the Tri-Loom, so we recruited her to work against them. She may one day make a fine agent. Ah, if only I could have shared this joyous news under more auspicious circumstances."

"Oh!" said Mrs. Gaunt, going to the car and reaching in to fetch her handbag. "Lady Hortensia is here! She'll want to say hello." She went over to pass the cat in the handbag up to her daughter, who unzipped the bag and took the rather bedraggled-looking cat out to cradle.

"Hello, Lady Hortensia," Miss Gaunt said. "You appear to be unharmed. There are bullet holes in that motorcar, so that is a relief. I would be unhappy if you were hurt at all."

Father leaned in. "What's going on, son?"

"That's Mr. Gaunt's daughter," I whispered back. "Mr. Scant's niece. She was supposed to be a hostage."

"I am a hostage," she said, who had her uncle's sharp ears. "Father still owes seventeen thousand five hundred and six pounds for my release, less any payments since my last update."

"But . . . my darling, you're here. You're walking free."

"I am here. Not free. Tomorrow I will be in Paris

again. On Friday, Berlin. We may have captured these Tri-Loom associates, but there are at least six hundred and fifty more in Europe. If I am not back in Paris tomorrow, they will send assassins."

"Who are the Tri-Loom?" I asked.

"A Chinese crime syndicate," said Dr. Mikolaitis. "They are what the Lice dream they could be. Many times bigger, and with real power."

"Father's debt was transferred from the Wood-houselee Society to the Tri-Loom. They are the ones to whom Father owes his debt," said Elspeth.

"Ellie, my sweet child!" Mr. Gaunt held up his arms imploringly. "We can protect you."

"And if it's money you need, I can help," said Father.

"The money must come from my father," said Miss Scant. "From his own earnings. That is very important to me."

"Ellie, at least let me hold you again," said Mrs. Gaunt. "I have been so worried."

Miss Cai laughed. "You don't have to worry about *Ellie*!"

Miss Gaunt nodded. "We will have time for embraces later. For now, we need to take these criminals somewhere safe. I also have an apple I would like to eat. Most urgently, more hostile combatants are approaching from the mausoleum."

She was right: though still far off, a considerable number of men were on the move. Miss Cai hurried to the roadside and whistled for the horses. The one that had reared up had not been shot, only taken fright, and both animals were well-trained enough to come trotting back.

Young man?" said Miss Gaunt.

"I . . . yes?" I answered.

"Please take Lady Hortensia. She is still quite afraid."

"Oh. Yes, all right."

"And now we should all escape."

"Into the motorcar!" said Father. "Come on, Son."

Tearfully, Mrs. Gaunt called out one final time, "Write to us, Ellie, won't you?"

Elspeth Gaunt looked over as she heaved Mr. Binns onto the back of her horse. "Yes. I suppose I *could* do that."

"We love you," said Mr. Gaunt as he led his wife away and to the motorcar. With Mr. Scant and Dr. Mikolaitis again clinging to the outside of the motorcar, Mrs. George eased us forward. One tire had been shot and let out an alarming groan, but we were mobile. We edged around the inert land ironclad and were on our way.

"Now then, Mr. Scant—I think I'm well over-due your explanation," said Father, leaning out of the window to address his valet.

"Yes, sir. Well, it began with two boys much in love with science . . ."

And so Mr. Scant told the story of our adven-ture, leaving out a good deal of the details and—after first casting me as an innocent, drawn along for leverage—letting me tell Father however much I wanted to. And I wanted to tell him everything. Mr. Gaunt grew increasingly sullen as the tale reached its triumphant ending, and he eventually spoke up: "Yes—but this isn't over, is it? There are going to be consequences after this. Even forgetting China, Binns certainly had friends in his wretched club too. We didn't do away with the whole lot of them. And whoever Ellie is working for, at some point they'll have to hand Binns to Scotland Yard, and don't be surprised if some strings are pulled and no charges stick."

"Ah, well, that is where *this* comes into play," Mr. Scant said, drawing out a small case.

"What have you got there?" said Father.

"Film. From a camera that we had in the balloon. I was very careful to take it out under the cover of the fireworks. You see, on this film, there is a lovely, clear image of Mr. Binns wearing a certain claw. It may even show his wife by his side with some very unladylike pistols."

"Nothing unladylike about pistols," Mrs. George trilled.

"The point is," Mr. Scant went on, "that the newspapers will be *very* keen to print this. The gentlemen we were dealing with may persuade the police to turn a blind eye, but the newspapers? Oh, that is another matter. We'll send it to them, and if Mr. Binns comes back, the world will be against him. And should one of his respectable friends turn nasty, well, I'm sure we can find a picture of the man looking chummy with our new Claw, and they'll understand the situation."

"I said from the beginning you're a clever egg, Scant," said Father. "And you, Son—never knew you had it in you. I want to give you a good whack for putting yourself in harm's way, but maybe you're old enough now to make you own choices. I'm proud of you. Once we're home, Scant, I'll have you explain it again—can't say I took it all in with you out the window there—but by the looks of this, I'd say we won!"

"We haven't won until our Ellie is back with us," said Mrs. Gaunt.

"I promise you, Winifred, we will get through everything together," Mr. Scant said.

"All of us," I said. I looked to Father to see if he would forbid it, but he simply gave a slow nod.

"All well and good," came a distant-sounding voice, "but do you think I could swap places with somebody at some point?"

The four of us on the backseat turned to look at Dr. Mikolaitis, who didn't look very comfortable hanging to the back of the motorcar.

"If it's convenient . . ."

Epilogue

I would be lying if I said the thought hadn't struck me even before we reached home that day.

When I finally plucked up the courage to ask my question, almost two weeks later, "What do you mean, Master Oliver?" was Mr. Scant's response.

"Well . . . the battle is over, isn't it? You don't need to steal art back from Mr. Binns. Mr. Gaunt even got all the credit for the photos exposing the 'Real Claw.'"

"Indeed."

It had been a fine day when the newspapers printed our photograph of Mr. and Mrs. Binns, along with a full story of a raid on their house that uncovered numerous strange trinkets and an array of stolen goods even Mr. Scant had not known about.

Scotland Yard announced it had the Binnses in custody, and the press named Reginald Gaunt as the intrepid Beards and Binns employee who felt honor-bound to expose his employer. Poor old Mr. Beards had been in a sorry state, with his company suddenly infamous, until Father negotiated a takeover by Diplexito Engineering and Combustibles Ltd., Tunbridge Wells. And just as the company was preparing to branch out into airships.

Christmas had arrived, and I had a new bike to learn to ride, at least as soon as the ground began to thaw. Out daydreaming about routes around the garden, I went to visit Mr. Scant in the Ice House.

"I just don't see why you're still here," I said to Mr. Scant. "Now that it's all . . . come together, you don't have any reason to be serving Father."

"Ah. Is the idea troubling you, Master Oliver?"

"You and your brother can go back to being scientists."

Mr. Scant stopped tinkering with the contraption he was working on and went to sit on his rocking chair. He had salvaged every small part of the old chair and built a new one around them. In a way, it was still the old rocking chair, very heavily restored. "We *could*," he said.

"So why are you still at Father's side? Is it only until you pay him back?"

"For the traction engine?" Mr. Scant smiled, something he had been doing a lot more often. "No, I could repay him for that in my own way. But the truth is that I don't want things to change so dramatically. Especially now that Reggie can come and visit whenever he pleases. I rather like it here. I am very good at being a gentleman's gentleman. You also ought to hesitate before thinking everything has been tied up with a bow. Life is seldom so tidy. If Binns escapes, or sends his son, or someone we have ruined by our actions comes looking for revenge, I should like to meet him with the people I trust. The people I have around me here. There's also the matter of young Elspeth Gaunt, who so far hasn't sent word to her mother and father of her whereabouts, or anything else. Thinking of her and her young friend, we may have made an enemy of some particularly worrisome people out in China."

"If anything happens, I hope you'll let me help you."

"Of course, Master Oliver. You are still, after all, my apprentice."

I smiled. "I'm glad to hear it."

"We'll have to keep your father in the dark, I think—though he does seem to be paying more attention to you now."

"Yes," I replied. "It's a bit odd."

"Well, as long as we don't tell any outright lies, I think there's still some more good we can do in this world. And I need to work to restore my reputation as a man who tells no lies. I hope you have forgiven me my indiscretions."

"I have. But there's still one thing."

"Yes?"

"You told me that your real name isn't Hector. Was that a lie?"

Mr. Scant stopped rocking. "Strictly, no."

"But Mr. Gaunt—he calls you 'Heck.'"

Mr. Scant looked embarrassed, another new sign of humanity. "My name was *meant* to be Hector. Unfortunately, my father was the one left to submit it at the registry. He wasn't one for details, and nor was the registry official. So on my birth certificate, I am *Ector*. No *H*. And if you laugh, the partnership is off."

He watched me, and I watched him. And then it was too late. "I'm sorry!" I cried. "I can't help it!"

On a reconstructed platform above us, the claw

I had worn sat on a little table, untouched since we first placed it there. The connection between Mr. Scant and the Ruminating Claw had been broken. The true identity of the Claw would only ever be known to our small circle, and perhaps to certain secret societies. The rest of the world would associate the claw with Mr. Binns and his misdeeds. There was another claw, of course; the strange, misshapen one made of scraps and pipes, and that I kept in my room as a memento of sorts, even though Meg and Penny often whispered about it and laughed. Chudley came over for a visit one Saturday, and when he saw it, he nodded sadly and said it was a modernist sculpture expressing heartache and rejection. "It takes an artist's eye to see these things, you know," he said with a doleful expression.

Mrs. George never spoke again of the events at the mausoleum, but I suspected she looked at Mr. Scant in a whole new way—and she had begun making orders in person from a butcher's across town, just to keep an eye on the owners' larger-than-life daughter. One day, Mrs. George received delivery of a cooking pot that seemed to have been crudely hammered out of a sheet of bronze—such as might once have served as a breastplate.

The day after we came home from the mauso-leum, Mr. Ibberts had given Father a note of resigna-tion. In his late years, he had discovered a great desire to teach abroad, he said. When last we heard of him, he was eager to visit Canada. As Mother began look-ing for a replacement, I wondered what she would think of a Lithuanian tutor with a doctorate, one who happened to be searching for a new job himself.

As for Father himself, he still had little time to spare, but now he occasionally went so far as to pat my shoulder or tell me about the news he was read-ing in his morning paper. Mother told me he had been considering taking me to the company during the school holidays, a development she mentioned as if it were the most exciting thing that had ever hap-pened in my life. But then, she had thought I'd be thrilled by ballet, too.

Through that crisp and peaceful winter, I often thought about the future. It was a beautiful thing—the best part of it being the number of lives I would be able to live. As many as I wanted. Because if Mr. Scant had taught me anything, it was that a person needn't settle for just one.

Acknowledgments

Thank you to my supportive friends and family. Life is about having fun, and the world would be a dreary place without you.

Thank you to my editor, Greg Hunter at Lerner, for your immediate understanding of everything I hoped someone would one day understand.

Thank you to Fiona Kenshole at Transatlantic Literary Agency, effortlessly lighting up the most daunting of paths with her boundless enthusiasm.

Thank you to Richard Sala for being so readily able to paint the inside of my head.

Thank you to my teachers, especially Anne Barton—may you rest in peace, Professor. I wish I'd spent more time listening to your stories, though I don't regret for one moment all that time we spent chasing your cats.

Thank you to James Wills—an hour of your time improved the book tenfold.

And of course, thank you to my readers, for taking a chance on this new, untested author—or possibly, if I'm lucky, for going back to see where this old hack's journey began.

About the Author

Bryan Methods grew up in a tiny village south of London called Crowhurst. He studied English at Trinity College, Cambridge, and has been working on a PhD on First World War poets. He currently lives in Tokyo, Japan, where he loves playing in bands, fencing, and video games.

COMING IN 2017

BOOK II

In the next stirring installment, Mr. Scant and Oliver arrive in Paris, searching for Elspeth Gaunt. They soon discover that children are disappearing, snatched from the streets. Guided by a young Parisian whose brother was taken, Mr. Scant and Oliver follow the trail of clues to Shanghai, where they unravel a plot to overthrow the Emperor of China himself. Can Mr. Scant and his allies foil the conspiracy and rescue the children, or will they fall victim to a shadowy criminal organization bent on international war? And where in all this is Elspeth Gaunt?

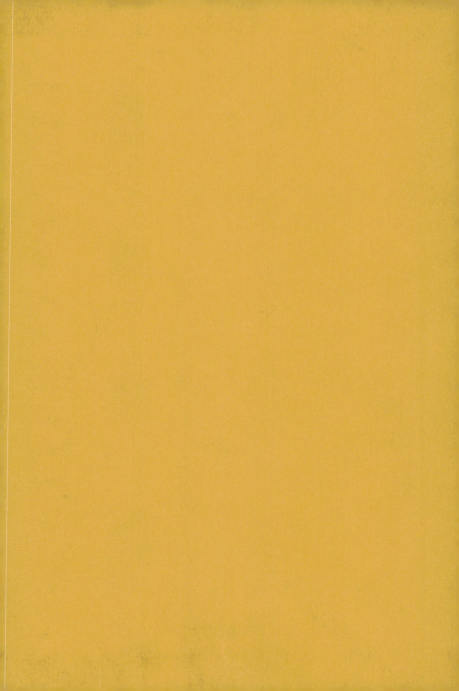